The HALLOWEEN Book

The Halloween Book

a novella by Juno Jakob

This paperback edition First Published in Great Britain in 2021 by Beercott Books.

Beercott Books

www.beercottbooks.co.uk

Thinking of:
Ray Bradbury

Contents

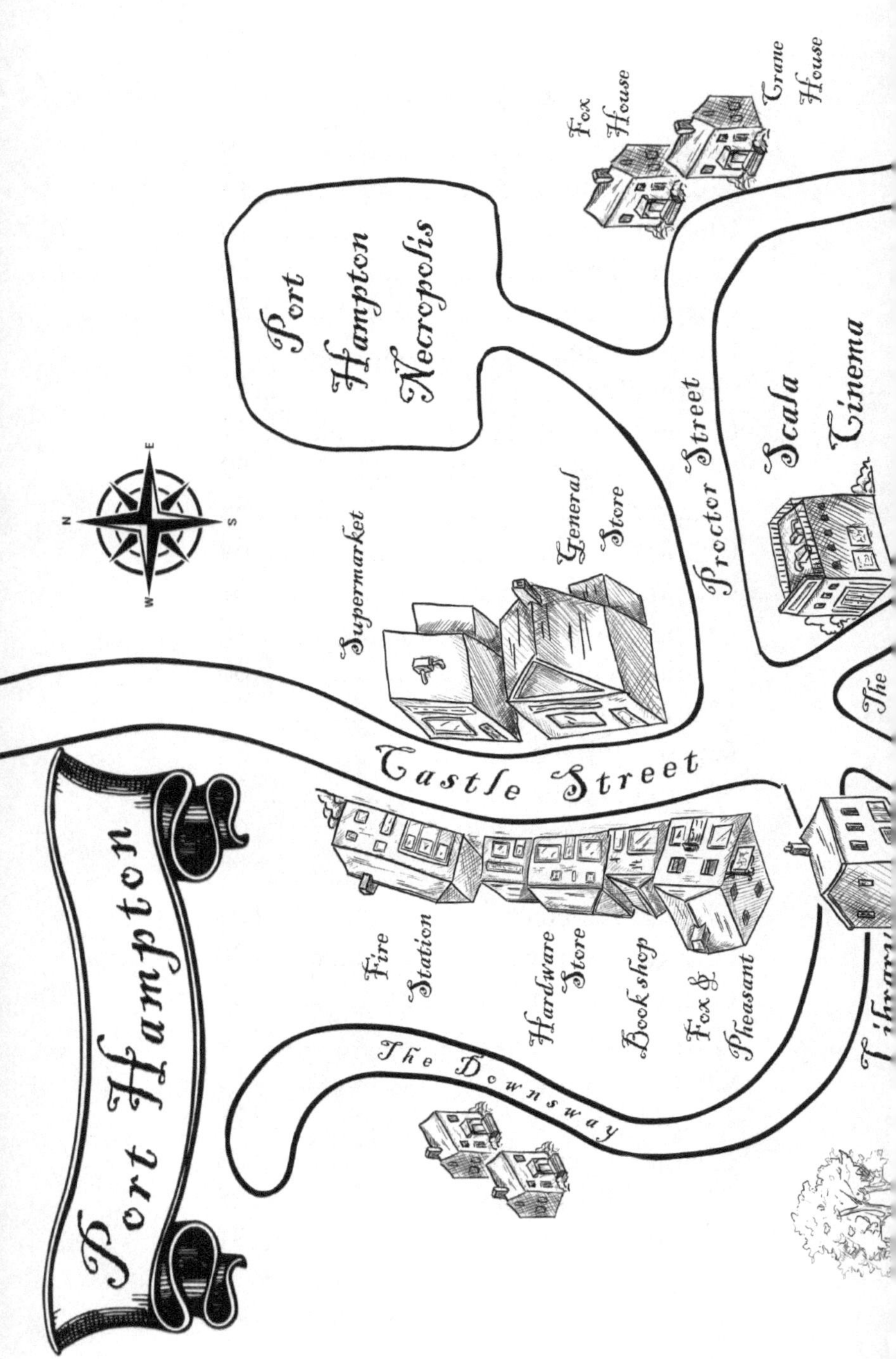

Port Hampton
Fox House
Crane House
Port Hampton Necropolis
Supermarket
General Store
Proctor Street
Scala Cinema
Castle Street
The
Fire Station
Hardware Store
Bookshop
Fox & Pheasant
Library
The Downsway
N
E
S
W

Meadow Bank Lake
Hospital Lane
Mortuary
Doctors Surgery
White Hart Lane
Castle Street
Town Hall
Castle
The Den
Church
The Vicarage

PROLOGUE

If you were to drive south of the city of Crowthrone, Hampshire, taking the third exit on the Talbot roundabout, then the fifteen-minute drive through the wooded St. Helena Way, you would reach the sleepy little town of Port Hampton.

The town was surrounded on three sides by the Pembury Forest and farmland and the most southern side faced out toward the ocean. Between the deep blue sea and the town stood Port Hampton castle, a Roman era fort that now lay in weathered ruins. The castle was full of the town's history; from the heroic battles with knights and soldiers to the dark side of the 1690 witchcraft trials, the events that gave the town its peculiar reputation.

Running through the heart of the town was Castle Street, where there was everything you needed to live a simple life; a well-stocked library, a police and fire station (including the traditional Dalmatian), a well-liked doctor who was always kind when injection time came around, the *Hawthorne Mortuary* handled the dearly departed residents while Reverend Blair of the church dealt with the services and lead the departed away. *The Fox & The Pheasant* was where the town's people drank in the evenings while discussing the recent gossip. *Taylor's' Hardware* catered for all your D.I.Y needs while Mr. Raimi ran the general store which sold everything from art supplies to toys for Christmas. *Otters* bookstore was where your literary adventures could be bought, and *Bennett's & Co* sold all kinds of wonderful food and drinks.

Spreading out from Castle Street were the roads and streets where the kind townsfolk lived in peaceful houses. Each person with their own thoughts, fears, and memories. Everyone knew their neighbour and their neighbours knew them.

Port Hampton. A peaceful, kind, and happy place.

A town where wonderful things happened in the bright sunlight of Summer, where strange things happened in the dusk of Autumn, where beautiful things happened in the night of Winter and humble things happened in the blooming of Spring.

Today was a special day, perhaps the most special.

October Thirty-First, 1992.

Halloween.

CHAPTER ONE

The October evening air was charged. It was full of spooky goings on, magic, wishes, macabre grins and bright moonlight. Children of all ages were dressing in all manner of scary costumes becoming creatures of the night, just for this one wonderful night.

The special night of Halloween.

Maya Fox, aged ten years old, sat waiting on her front porch. She could see all the other kids trick or treating and worried that all the good treats would be gone before she and Henry could get there.

She yelled out at the house next door.

"Come on, Henry!" she cried.

There was a muted cry from next door and then, like a bolt of lightning, Henry Crane, aged eleven years old, came running down the front steps and then up onto Maya's porch. He was dressed like a chilling skeleton, skull and all. White felt stitched on black cotton.

"How do I look?" he asked, holding out his arms.

"Very scary. And me?" Maya asked, pulling down her mask. The hideous face of a witch, complete with a long glitter covered cape and tall black pointed hat.

"We make a gruesome twosome," chuckled Henry.

The echoes of a hundred children calling 'Trick or Treat' hung on the darkness around them. Beckoning them.

"Let's go! You took so long I doubt there's anything left out there," said Maya, bounding down the front steps two at a time.

"Trick or treat!" the two friends called, holding out their pillow sacks. The kind faced old woman that opened the decorated door before them smiled as she handed down an orange bucket full to the brim with fun sized chocolate bars. Maya and Henry both took one with thanks and added it to their bounty of sweets.

And so, for the next hour, the two of them climbed stairs to front porches and chimed 'Trick or Treat'. They were given all kinds of sweet candies and treats and, on one occasion, old man Mr. Kregg said 'Trick' when they knocked on his front door. Henry did a handstand and was rewarded with a full bar of *Bennett's & Co* white chocolate and two gummy worms.

As they walked back to the street, they allowed

themselves the treat of breathing in the October air. It had a smoky taste and feel. It smelt like nothing else during the whole year, completely unique to the month of October. The streetlights, the ones that had been on since five in the evening, shone brightly, giving all the trick or treaters wandering the streets a glow, cutting them out of the flat night around them. Only in October could you see dozens and dozens of bright pumpkin faces staring off front porches and behind front windows. This night was precious and rare, a once-a-year experience. It was a child's dream not a nightmare. Walking the haunted streets made you feel just like your costume, full of fright and laughter.

Jim Hall, a spaceman and Rob Zimmerman, dressed as a spider with multiple legs suspended with twine, came running up the street, their treat bags over their shoulders ready to burst.

"Hi, guys!" Jim greeted.

"Geez," Henry was astounded. "Where did you get all that?"

"We went to Mrs. Myers! She's giving out full sized chocolate," Jim said, out of breath and pulling open his pillow sack.

Full sized chocolates were the holy grail of Halloween night, the thing you always hoped for but rarely saw.

Zimmerman, or as the other kids called him, Zimmy, lifted his mask to breath in the cool night air. "I hear over on White Hart Lane there is a guy giving out cookies! The chewy kind."

Maya squeaked with excitement. "Let's go there now!"

"That's where we're headed," said Zimmy, dropping his mask back down.

The four friends ran down the street, each hauling their heavy bags full of treats that only taste good and sweet on Halloween night. It was always sweeter and richer on that special night.

On the corner of White Hart Lane was the town hall, which looked void of all decorations except a single window decal of a giant smiling pumpkin. Inside, the school's headmaster, Mr. Raynham, was judging this year's costume contest and although the place was dark, the sound of children cheering could be heard. The winner of the costume contest got a whole months' worth of sweets as a prize, as well as a giant blue ribbon to proudly display until next Halloween.

Maya and Henry had decided to simply trick or treat instead of wasting time at the contest. It had been just last year that Henry himself had won first place for his ghoulish zombie costume. Why, if they hit enough houses tonight instead, they would easily get two months' worth of candy if the night was right and proper.

"Look, let's cut down here! We'll get there quicker," Jim yelled, running down the little alley between Proctor Street and White Hart Lane.

Maya stopped in her tracks, looking at the dark and weathered house at the opposite end of the alley.

Henry turned to her as Zimmy and Jim ran off with cheer and vigour.

"What's wrong?" asked Henry.

Maya pointed to the house. "That's Kelly Krug's house…"

Kelly Krug. The biggest bully in the whole of Port Hampton, except maybe Tobe Green. Maya and Henry were not the only victims of that terrible twosome. Many days on the playground were spent hiding from Kelly and Tobe. How many times had Henry rushed to the milk lines so he could spend his milk money before Kelly got it and Tobe Green would come stalking and stick wet fingers in kid's ears until they screamed? They picked on pretty much every kid in school and were always in detention for it.

Bullies, simple as that.

Maya looked nervously at the intimidating house.

Henry could see his friend's fear. "Look, we'll just quickly run through here and bolt down the street. Zimmy and Jim have already got past it with no problems."

Maya tried to move her feet, which felt set in concrete, but it was only with the pull of her hand that she began to walk. She clutched her pillow sack tightly in her small hand but knew it could be snatched at any minute by Kelly if the bully suddenly leapt from the shadows.

It still came as a surprise when Kelly Krug emerged from the other end of the alley. She was a big girl with broad shoulders, a mop of dark greasy hair and her mouth smeared with chocolate, which had no doubt been stolen from other kids.

"Ah it's you two! Likkle Maya and Henry. Where you been picking sweets from?" Kelly snatched the pointed witch's hat from Maya's head and stomped on it with a heavy foot.

"We're…" Maya began, feeling the sickly feeling of fear in her throat. "We're trick or treating."

Kelly laughed while Henry tried to step between the bully and his friend.

"You don't trick or treat Maya, you beg 'cause your family is poor. You're a little beggar."

"Come on Krug, let us past," Henry tried to sound brave but knew Kelly was almost twice his weight and nearly two years older.

A hand came from behind and snatched Henry's pillow sack away. Whirling around, Henry saw the mean grin of Tobe Green. A boy with a wicked face and dark eyes.

"What have we here then?" said Tobe, dipping a hand into the sack.

"Give it back!" Henry yelled, trying to snatch the bag from Tobe's hand.

"Ah, ah, ah, there's a tax for walking through my alley. I'm gonna have to take half of your sweets," Tobe explained viciously, grabbing a huge handful of treats and shoving it into his hoody pocket.

Kelly reached into Maya's bag and took large handfuls of chocolates.

Maya wanted to fight back but her fear was too great. She had been on the end of Kelly's slaps and punches too often. She would never be able to fight off Kelly.

"Can we go now?" asked Henry, both annoyed and angry, snatching his sack back.

"Sure, but remember, if you walk through again you have to pay the taxes," Tobe and Kelly laughed before disappearing back out of the alley.

Though the tears welled in Maya's eyes, she held them back. They were not simply tears of sadness over losing her precious Halloween treats. They were tears of anger and shame. Kelly Krug and Tobe Green had beaten her and she hated it with all her mind and soul. She simply wouldn't give them the satisfaction of her tears.

Henry sighed and looked down into his now half empty bag. "Come on, Maya. Let's go see what's left on White Hart Lane. Maybe there's still some good stuff. Then we'll go home and watch *Charlie Brown*'.

They arrived back at Maya's house (after getting some full-sized chocolate bars from Mrs. Myers) and sat defeated on the front porch, listening to the television inside playing a scary movie. The screams floating across the airwaves and echoing in the empty trees.

Henry tipped both pillow sacks out onto the wooden boards, pooling their candy hauls together.

"There we go! Now we at least have a good haul," said Henry, spreading the chocolate and gummy sweets out to see all the different labels and brands.

Though there was plenty of treats in front of her, Maya preferred the treat that couldn't be seen or eaten. A truly beautiful treat.

The mysterious, spooky, macabre chill of Halloween night. The smells of bonfires, pumpkin pie and roaming spirits walking the streets amongst the costumed living. The chill seeped into her body, both warm like the flame inside a Jack-O'-Lantern and cold like a fresh, deep grace in some eerie cemetery. The October chills were nowhere else in the rest of the year and it seemed only the children of the town were able to sense them.

The air was magical and the possibilities were endless.

She took a full-sized chocolate bar and tore it open.

Henry took another.

"Happy Halloween Maya," Henry said, tapping her bar with his own.

A toast.

"Happy Halloween Henry," Maya smiled back, missing a front baby tooth.

The wind blew the dead leaves up into the air where they were carried off into the darkness.

CHAPTER TWO

Now that it was November, Halloween and all its special charm was another full three hundred and sixty-five days away, though there were still remains of the holiday littered on the streets: candy wrappers, old Jack-O'-Lanterns, ripped streamers and the odd discarded mask laying alone on the damp ground staring up at the grey sky. The right nose could pick up the smell of pumpkins, just before they started to rot.

The children of the town awoke with the tingle of pride knowing they had celebrated Halloween the right way.

Today, being a Sunday, was a chore day and there was one chore on a Sunday they couldn't hide or run from.

Church.

Church. The most boring and agonizing hour of the weekend. First it was waking up early (on a weekend, no less), followed by dressing in what the parents called 'Sunday Best Clothes', which were always itchy and uncomfortable, then it was the walk, where along the way all the adults would stop and talk about adult things while the children were teased with the prospect of playing on a Sunday. The final challenge was sitting in those hard wooden pews while the Reverend Blair thumped his bible and spat about wickedness and sinners of the world in the freezing cold church.

Henry felt he already led a good life. He was a good boy. He didn't steal or cheat or hurt people, so he didn't see why old man Blair was saying he was a sinner and needed to ask for forgiveness for something he didn't do.

Church. Even the word filled Henry Crane with dread.

As he sat on the bottom step, wrestling with his shoelaces on the shiny shoes that gave him blisters, Henry could already hear his father, Bruce, talking about how important it was to go to church every Sunday.

"It gives us guidance in our day-to-day life," was a phrase Henry had heard every Sunday for most of his life.

"And the good Reverend Blair knows his stuff. I bet he could read the bible with his eyes closed, probably has the whole thing memorized," Bruce theorized, adjusting his tie in the hallway mirror.

Grandpa Ray, snowy haired and wise, had a different view as he hobbled on his cane into the hall. "Ah, the Hell with Blair. He's as bad as the rest of us."

"Dad, come on," Carol Crane said, getting their coats from under the stairs. "It's only an hour a day, not even a day. An hour a week."

"I'd be better off here," said Grandpa Ray. "Me and Henry can stay here, and you can just tell us what happened when you get back. Give us the abridged version."

Grandpa Ray shot his grandson a cheeky wink.

It was the same playful argument every week. Grandpa Ray wanted to stay at home and read his books with his coffee but always ended up going along to keep his daughter happy.

Though he may have been approaching eighty years old, he still had the energy and wit of a thousand boys. Always had a joke for the right moment and it always hit home. He had stories that filled the evenings, stories from all over the world and things he had done. He was never one to turn down a good board game or even a simple game of *Go Fish*.

It was always Grandpa Ray who had been so excited when he saw the Halloween decorations and costumes in the shops for the first time of any given year. It has been Grandpa Ray who took Henry out to the pumpkin patch to gather the biggest and best pumpkins for Jack-O'-

Lanterns. It was always Grandpa Ray, full of spirit and joy, handing out sweets to trick or treaters and complimenting every costume that came to the door. Grandpa Ray might be the only person on the whole planet who loved Halloween as much as Henry and Maya. His excitement for Halloween was enormous and infectious.

Grandpa Ray was truly The October Man.

Leaning on his cane, Grandpa Ray put his hand on his grandson's shoulder. "Come on then Henry, let's get this over with."

They all donned their coats and stepped out into the surprisingly chilly morning.

Next door, Maya ran down her porch steps and joined the Cranes, just like she did every first Sunday of the month while her mother, Dawn Fox, slept in after working the night shift.

They all began to walk, and Henry and Maya fell a few steps back.

"Did you have a belly ache this morning?" she asked.

Henry shook his head. "Nah, I got a belly of lead, nout can make me sick… except maybe Reverend Blair."

The children giggled, as did Grandpa Ray.

"I think I have enough sweets to last a week," Maya estimated.

"I think I have two days' worth at max," Henry laughed.

The leaves on the floor, though now void of their spooky feel, were still a delight to kick through, until Henry's mother told him to stop scuffing his good shoes.

It was ice cold in the church, as usual. As the crowd slowly moved deeper into the building, moving into pews exchanging hellos and pleasantries, Maya and Henry looked around for the other kids, who could also think of better things to do on a Sunday.

There was Jim Hall but no Zimmy (Zimmy went to the synagogue in Crowthrone on a Saturday), a few rows further back were Hunter Tapert and Cathy Campbell. Charlotte May looked pretty with a blue bow in her red hair. Dylan Samuel was staring at the ceiling, no doubt counting down the seconds until he could leave. Even Kelly Krug had been dragged to church by her mother and was sat wearing a very ugly dress. Tobe Green and Billy Wallace were in the back row whispering. It seemed no kid had been spared the torture of church.

As the hush came over the congregation, a pretty dark-haired girl approached the pulpit at the front of the room. It was Elizabeth Blair, the Reverend's daughter. Though she attended the same school as most of the kids, they hardly knew her. She was often found sitting alone on the playground, her nose in a book. She was always thought of as the weird, quiet kid who never got into trouble.

Elizabeth led the church folk in the Lord's prayer, which all the adults followed while the children simply mumbled along. Her voice was pretty and clear, and the grown-ups were always doting over her, saying why couldn't they have kids like Elizabeth Blair.

With less than an hour to go, the boredom was already setting in for Maya and Henry. There was a good leaf pile in the back garden which was just ready for jumping headfirst into.

When Elizabeth had finished the prayer and the adults had stopped clapping. HE stepped up to the pulpit.

Reverend Hugh Blair was a large man. His broad shoulders were topped with a long face that always appeared to be frowning. His eyeglasses perched on the end of his bulbous nose and his sharp eyes seemed to cut right through souls. He may be the boring man slamming the bible, but there was no doubt in the children's minds, Blair was a scary man.

"Welcome my friends, on this glorious Sunday morning," his deep voice boomed in the room, making everyone sit up straight. "We come here to celebrate our love for God in his house. But today I have something troubling to tell you about. Something that has been troubling me a great deal."

He rapped his fat fingers against the pulpit, his angry eyes on his flock.

Someone coughed lightly in the crowd, Blair's eyes shot in the direction of the culprit.

"You all know what I am talking about..." Blair said slowly.

Henry felt himself slip into the familiar feeling of church, a feeling of sagging down and letting the sound of Blair's voice wash over him. Henry was simply trying to work out how quickly he could do his chores and get out to play. If he tried, he could get a whole afternoon of play. He knew his friend Maya was thinking the same thing.

A single word made Henry near jump from the pews, and it grabbed his attention like a vigilant owl catching a running mouse.

"...I am talking about this Halloween," Blair said firmly.

Henry, Maya and even Grandpa Ray sat on the edge of their pews.

"Last night, I saw children dressed as demons and devils. Running around in their unholy and ridiculous costumes. How can we allow such blasphemy? How can we let the children of this town act in such a way? This Devil's day goes against the teaching of our Lord, Jesus Christ."

Henry could feel the concern growing within him. Maya reached out a sweaty hand for his. They held each other tight.

"We only need to look back in our town history to see this Devil's day has continued for too long. 1690, the year of our witchcraft trials," Blair reminded. "Those heretics executed here are a smear on our good town. A smear on our history. This Halloween our children are so fond of is the witch's day! It's for those witches! Witches buried in this very churchyard, I'm sorry to say."

Every kid in town had learnt about the witchcraft trials of 1690. In history class at school, the teacher told dark stories of men and women, twenty in all, being hung at the castle for supposedly bewitching the children of the town. The trials brought tourism money to Port Hampton and there were reminders of them all over the little town: a museum, t-shirts for sale, a stone memorial in the town's triangle beneath the grand oak tree, even the one police car in town had a witch riding a broom on it. There were books and films made about the trials. Some even called Port Hampton 'England's Salem'.

"Now, I know most of you are good honest people, people who still believe in coming to

God's house to celebrate his love and kindness and rid ourselves of sins. The Devil's day destroys our way of life and throws children into all sorts of occult and blackness. We can no longer expose them to such things. They should grow up knowing the Lord's love," Blair growled, his eyes wide.

Henry sat in disbelief, feeling personally insulted. He squeezed Maya's hand tightly.

Some of the adults were nodding along with Blair's words. Some even clapping.

"We need to rid ourselves of such wicked and wrong ways. Halloween is an abomination!" He slammed a holy fist on the pulpit.

Adults cheered and agreed.

"You're hurting my hand," Maya whispered.

Henry could barely contain his anger as the Reverend continued his speech. Who was he to talk about special and wonderful Halloween? Adults didn't understand it, except Grandpa Ray, of course.

Behind him, Henry heard a cough. He turned and saw Mr. Raimi, the general store owner, who was young and bearded, stand as a lone figure. He stood against the heavy silence and stared at Blair, who looked like he would never give into a staring match.

Mr. Raimi simply and quietly stepped out into

the aisle and silently walked out of the church. A complete act of defiance.

"Well, I can see we have someone who disagrees," Blair began.

"You're damn right!" called out Grandpa Ray, his face bright red.

The church gave a collected gasp.

"Dad!" Carol cried out, putting a hand on him.

Grandpa Ray brushed her off. "Nah, to Hell with this."

Henry was filled with pride for his grandfather.

Blair simply spoke louder, covering the commotion from the pews. "It is now my duty, my duty delivered from our Lord, to rid our town of Halloween and I call on all of you to support it."

CHAPTER THREE

Grandpa Ray pushed through the front door and hobbled in on his cane, his face redder than ever.

"I can't believe the guff of that guy," he cried, falling into his usual armchair. "The absolute nerve of the guy. Who does he think he is?! Huh?"

"Oh Dad, come on, settle down," Carol said, closing the front door and taking off her church hat.

"No. The man's a nut!" Grandpa Ray protested.

"Now, dad, you know you overreact to things. Just let it go," said Carol.

"Who in Hell does he think he is to ban Halloween?" he asked, not looking for an answer.

"Well, maybe he has a point," Bruce said, undoing his tie.

Henry and Maya took off their shoes and waited in the hallway, listening intently to the adults. Henry felt it was his duty to stand up for defenceless Halloween, but suspected Grandpa Ray could hold up his own in an argument.

"Henry my boy, go get your grandpa the whiskey bottle. I need a stiff drink," sighed Grandpa Ray, tossing his cane down in anger.

Henry got the whiskey from the sideboard. He knew that grandpa was really angry when he asked for the bottle. Not that he drank a lot but when it's only eleven thirty on a Sunday morning and he's drinking, it must mean he was pretty ticked off.

Bruce walked into the living room and sat down on the sofa. "Blair spoke a lot of truth too, Ray. All that stuff about being against the Lord…"

"He's just a bible nut who thinks he knows what to do," Grandpa Ray waved a hand.

"And so what if we don't celebrate Halloween anymore. Do you really think it's a big deal?" Bruce asked.

"Yes!" Henry found himself yelping.

"Henry, don't butt into conversations," his mother corrected.

He didn't apologize.

Carol pushed the children out into the kitchen.

Grandpa Ray and Bruce continued to argue.

In the kitchen, Carol began to brew some

coffee while Maya had a glass of milk and Henry sulked.

"Why does Blair want to cancel Halloween?" Henry asked his mother, not touching his own glass of milk.

"It's nothing you need to worry about, Henry," she said, fussing with the coffee machine.

"But he wants to get rid of Halloween!" Henry cried. "Surely that needs to be talked about."

"Don't get smart Henry," Carol said with authority. "You're lucky you've had it for this long."

Henry quietened down and took a sip of milk.

Maya looked just as frustrated and upset.

Grandpa Ray came hobbling into the kitchen. A glass of whiskey in his free hand.

Bruce followed in, now in his slippers. "He makes good points. Halloween is such an American thing anyways. Why do we celebrate it?"

"Because it's goddamn fun!" replied Grandpa Ray before he gulped the remaining whiskey.

"Dad! Watch your mouth please," Carol said, eyeing the children.

"Look Ray, while you live under my roof, you follow our rules. We may not be completely honest, and we may not live by every word in the bible, but we are good Christians and I think Reverend Blair knows what's best for a good Christian family."

"And watch your mouth, Dad," Carol repeated.

Grandpa Ray looked at the other adults with disbelief. "I can't believe you agree with that madman! It's unheard of not celebrating Halloween in this day and age."

"Well maybe it's just time for a change. It would seem that we've been letting it go on for too long," said Bruce.

Grandpa Ray sat down at the table with the children and silence fell over the room.

"Now, I have to go and work on the car so I can get us all around," Bruce declared, rolling up his sleeves. "The tracking is terrible. Just keeps veering to the left."

"I'm going to change the beds," said Carol, following her husband out of the door.

When Carol and Bruce had left the room, Grandpa Ray leant in close to the children and spoke in whispers.

"You're good kids, aren't you?" he said.

Henry and Maya nodded.

"Now listen closely, really pay attention. I want you kids to make me a promise you hear?" Grandpa Ray smiled warmly.

Another nod from the children.

"You promise me you'll NEVER let Halloween die. Not ever. Do you understand?"

It was a promise that needn't be asked. Of course they wouldn't. Maya and Henry would do anything to save Halloween.

"I want you to both promise me right now, with all your heart and soul that you'll never let Blair win. You must keep Halloween."

Grandpa Ray held out his two pinkie fingers.

Maya was the first to wrap her own pinkie around his and Henry did the same.

"Promise," the three of them said in unison.

It was an unbreakable bond. The strongest of promises. The purest.

CHAPTER FOUR

The morning sun was out but the wind was chilled, and it rattled through the barren trees. Over the smooth planks of the front porch, Maya Fox spread out the remains of her and Henry's Halloween candy. Five chocolate bars (the full-sized bars were long gone), eighteen sour gummy worms, two candy apples, three bags of sherbet and a pack of mini marshmallows. All their wrappers were Halloween themed, so Maya still had the simple pleasure of a taste of October.

The screen door next door opened and slammed shut. Henry, with his usual red scarf around his neck, came walking towards her, hands stuffed in his jacket pocket.

"I'm blue. I need some of the good stuff," he said, climbing the porch steps.

Maya tugged a sour worm from the pile and offered it to him. He took it with a smile, knowing she had remembered his favourite. He bit off its head.

"How's your grandpa today?" Maya asked,

remembering the old man's promise they had made five days ago.

"He's calmed down a bit. He just sits smoking his pipe, looking out the window and only really speaking when I ask him something. I think he's just down at the moment," Henry explained. He hated seeing his grandpa so sad.

"He seemed pretty mad about Blair," observed Maya, opening the bag of marshmallows.

"Oh yeah, him and Dad had a big argument last night all about it. I honestly think Dad has been brainwashed by Blair. How else could someone possibly think Halloween should be banned?"

"How could he get brainwashed?" Maya asked.

"I don't know…" said Henry with uncertainty. "Maybe it's like some sort of secret television code or maybe something on the radio. It could be anything."

"Do you reckon it's all the adults?" Maya thought of her mother Dawn, who seemed unaffected by any brainwashing and had also commented negatively on Blair's strange plan

"No, I don't think so 'cause of Grandpa Ray. He doesn't want it banned. And Mr. Raimi walked right out in the middle of the speech, maybe he had some kind of strength against Blair?" Henry frowned, deep in thought.

"Do you think Mr. Raimi loves Halloween too?" asked Maya.

"How should I know? Maybe your mum knows. She's going out with him," Henry said.

He was right. Mr. Raimi (Maya had heard her mum call him Sam before) had been taking her mum out for dinners and evenings at the *Scala Cinema* for at least three months now. Mr. Raimi was often over for meals and evenings at the house. He was a fun, kind man and he seemed to make her mum happy and smile, something Maya always liked to see.

"I don't really speak to him though," said Maya "Sometimes he brings magic tricks to the house. He's a good magician."

Henry snapped his fingers in a Eureka moment. "Maybe it's something magic that stops Mr. Raimi being affected. That would make sense. And Grandpa Ray always said he wanted to be a magician when he grew up."

"Well, that must be it then," declared Maya.

The two children sat in silence, chewing on the remains of their treats, turning over their thoughts.

"What do you think the town will be like if there was no Halloween?" Henry finally asked.

"Oh," Maya shook her head from side to side. "I don't even want to imagine."

"No Jack-O'-Lanterns, no candy, no bedsheet ghosts, no ghoulish witches and monsters, no chilly October winds… can you honestly imagine?"

"Why it would be so plain and horrible. That night is made for all those things. There has to be a law down somewhere that says you MUST have pumpkin carving and scary movies on October thirty-first." Maya insisted.

"I don't know…Have you spoken with the others yet?" Henry asked.

"Not yet. Well, I spoke to Zimmy and he laughed about the whole thing but then the next day he came, and he said his parents had spoken with Kelly Krug's dad and they've now said they won't celebrate Halloween either."

"So, it's reaching out from the church," Henry was glum.

"Do you really think Blair could ban it?" Maya sounded fearful.

"I don't know," Henry was honest.

"What's he really so mad about anyways?" asked Maya.

Henry shrugged. "I can't see anything wrong with Halloween, certainly nothing that would get someone that… pissed off."

Maya giggled at the swear and looked over her

shoulder to make sure Mummy wasn't listening.

"I want to kick Reverend Blair in... the ass!" Maya yelled out and fell over laughing.

"Kick him right in his big fat ass!" Henry yelled at the top of his voice then fell back onto the porch holding his sides.

The two laughed and Grandpa Ray inside the house, sitting with his pipe and whiskey coffee heard then and he smiled.

CHAPTER FIVE

Raimi's General Store was quiet as Henry and Maya pushed their way through the door and out of the cold November weather. The bell chimed above the door. Mr. Raimi was standing behind the counter hunched over a clipboard taking inventory of his stock. To the right of the counter were the shelves that just a week before displayed all the wonderful Halloween decorations, now stuffed with Christmas decorations.

Maya turned down an aisle to look for the colouring book she wanted while Henry walked up to the counter pulling the rented video tapes from his backpack.

Mr. Raimi pushed aside his clipboard and smiled down at the little boy. "Good morning, Master Crane and how are we doing?"

"Fine. We have our videos to bring back," Henry said, placing the videos on the counter.

"Ah yes, the spooky marathon," Mr. Raimi remembered. "And how was it?"

Maya joined her friend. She carried a thick

book under her arm.

"It was great. I loved *Frankenstein*" said Maya. "And *The Creature from the Black Lagoon*, Oh and *The Phantom of the Opera*."

"Did you guys get nightmares?" Mr. Raimi chuckled. "These are the classic monsters, they used to give me nightmares growing up."

Henry shook his head, seeming distant as Mr. Raimi put the videos under the counter.

"And what about little Maya?" asked Mr. Raimi, beaming down at the young girl.

Maya looked down at her booted feet. "I only get them if it's a really scary movie."

"Ah such brave children. Is there anything else my two favourite customers need?" asked Mr. Raimi.

"Mummy says she'll be ready about seven tonight," Maya said with a mischievous smile. "Another smoochy date for you two."

"Yep," Mr. Raimi laughed. "Your mother is a very special lady, Maya."

Maya went shy and giggled.

The three stood in silence for a moment.

"How come you walked out?" Henry asked. "Why'd you walk out of church?"

Mr. Raimi put his hands on the counter and

looked down at the young boy. He paused as if selecting his words carefully. "Why do you think I left?"

"You don't like church?" Henry guessed.

"No. I don't hate church. Not when it's done right, I suppose."

"Is it Blair?" asked Maya.

"I suppose you could say that" Mr. Raimi said cryptically.

Henry looked up at the store owner. "What's his problem?"

Mr. Raimi sighed. "Well, I think Blair is the kind of guy who thinks he rules wide and well but his ideas aren't always the best."

"Like what else?" Henry pressed.

Mr. Raimi looked concerned for a moment. "Do you know what 'blackmail' means?"

Both children shook their heads.

"Ah, you'll find out when you're older," Mr. Raimi explained simply.

"Do you think he really wants to ban Halloween?" Maya asked.

"I think he's gonna try, yes," said Mr. Raimi.

Henry walked away from the counter and peered through the window at the church steeple poking out from among the grand oak trees across the street. "I don't think he'll do it. Not unless he can get the adults to agree."

Mr. Raimi let out a sigh. "From what the little birds tell me, he has Mayor Proctor's support already."

"What?!" The children yelp in unison.

"How true that is, I don't know," Mr. Raimi responded.

"My Grandpa Ray will never let it happen. My Grandpa is Mr. October." Henry said with pride.

"And here's me thinking I was Mr. October," laughed Mr. Raimi.

"My Grandpa knows all there is to know about Halloween."

"He does," Maya said, resting her elbows on the counter. "He tells us stories every night about Halloween when he was our age, like a million years ago."

"He's not that old!" Henry replied.

The bell above the door clinked as a customer walked in and their conversation went quiet.

Henry looked up hopefully but with eyes full of fear. "Do you think he'll really cancel it?"

Mr. Raimi looked at the children and with all honesty simply said. "I don't know, kids. I really don't know."

The two children looked downtrodden.

"Hey," Mr. Raimi began full of excitement. "Let me show you this new magic trick I learnt. See? Nothing in my hand…but look what's behind your ear, Maya!"

And from some magic place, the magician pulled a giant silver coin from behind the wonderstruck girl's ear. It lifted both Maya and Henry's spirits, even just for a moment.

The three friends giggled with glee and disbelief.

CHAPTER SIX

With the unstoppable force of time, the days after Halloween slipped by as autumn soon turned into winter. The nights grew longer and darker, hungry for daylight, eating away until darkness came by mid-afternoon. The wind, once warm to touch, became frosty and sharp. Rain became snow and the snow became ice and sleet. Footsteps cracked and shattered the frozen fallen leaves.

There were still three more special days before the year came to a close; Bonfire Night, Christmas and New Year's. Each day had its own wonderful senses.

Bonfire night had a smoky flavour and was burnt on the edges.

Christmas had a warm feeling and was frosted with decorations.

New Years was exciting and full of hope for the future.

The town of Port Hampton was putting 1992 to rest. It became a distant memory they recalled with fondness.

As spring began to bloom, littering the ground with new life and greenery, the people completely forgot about Blair and his bizarre ideas about Halloween. Blair had never mentioned it again and all was forgotten.

The town moved on with their lives and things returned to normal.

That was until May first, 1993.

Young Henry Crane's twelfth birthday…

CHAPTER SEVEN

On a bright, spring day, Henry was cycling at least two houses ahead of Maya and knew he would win the race. His bicycle was a new one for his birthday and Henry had given his old bike, which still had plenty of good miles on it, to his friend Maya.

Maya struggled to keep up.

"Come on, slow poke!" Henry called over his shoulder, feeling the breeze on his neck.

"I'm coming! I've never cycled before," Maya yelled, nearly out of breath.

The two of them turned down White Hart Lane with skidding tires and down Talbot Street away from the houses and towards the beginning of the blooming farmland surrounding the town.

Today might have been Henry's birthday but it was also the day Farmer Brown planted the new pumpkin plants that were destined to grow into swollen and large pumpkins ready for carving into chilling Jack-O'-Lanterns. They would grow and twist all over his land, and when the gates of the pumpkin patch opened on the first day of

October, Henry and Maya were sure they'd be the first ones through to get the very best pumpkins.

The five months would be a long wait.

The houses on each side of the children soon slipped away and they found themselves cycling along country roads, where the sun shone warm and bright high above them. Farmer Brown's farm was only about a mile from town, but was still a fair cycle for little legs.

As they reached the farm, the children skidded to a stop.

"Morning, Farmer Brown!" Henry called over the fence surrounding the farm.

The farmer waved a hand in the distance.

"How many pumpkins this year? Two or three hundred?" Maya yelled out, but not as loud as Henry.

The farmer kept working, hunched over, dipping the plants into the neatly ploughed ground.

"Do you think that many?" Maya asked Henry.

"Well, I don't know. It seemed like that last year. Do you know what face you're going to carve this year?" Henry asked, still watching the farmer.

"I try and do the same one each year," Maya said. "Triangle eyes and square teeth"

Henry scoffed. "That's a bit boring, don't you think?"

"I like to stay traditional. A classic face."

"Me and Grandpa Ray always sit and think of a new face. He knows how to carve the best pumpkin," Henry explained.

"Would you guys help me?" Maya asked.

"Of course! We could spend all of Halloween carving pumpkins. Squishing all those inner guts and seeds. Oh! And the smell too," Henry felt a shiver of pleasure recalling the feeling of pumpkin innards.

The farmer was moving closer to the fence, still dropping a few saplings every two feet or so as he moved slowly and evenly up the line. The farmer waved a hand at the kids.

"Come on Farmer Brown, how many pumpkins this year?" asked Maya.

Another wave.

"Why's he such a sour puss huh?" Henry asked his friend.

"I don't know. It's something to do with getting old, I think. My Grandma is the same," Maya said.

"Old people are always sour, except my Grandpa Ray," said Henry.

The farmer raised his head. "What y'all kids want?"

Henry cupped his hands and called out, even though the farmer was walking towards them. "How many pumpkins are you planting this year? Two or three hundred?"

The farmer wiped the sweat from the back of his neck. "None."

"What do you mean none?!" Henry asked, shocked.

"I ain't planting no pumpkins this year," the farmer said. "None."

"Why not?" Maya asked, climbing onto the fence.

"Just ain't," Farmer Brown explained flatly.

"But why?" Henry added quickly.

The farmer waved his hand again, dismissing their questions. "I do what I'm told and that's it."

And he began to walk back towards his house.

"What is Halloween without pumpkins though?" Henry called after the farmer, but his questions fell on deaf ears.

"No pumpkins?!" Maya stressed. "I've never heard of such a thing."

"Me neither," Henry replied quietly.

No pumpkins? No Jack-O'-Lanterns? Henry was hit with waves of both disbelief and sadness. A pumpkin was vital, maybe the most vital, part of Halloween. As far back as Henry could remember there had always been a bright, burning Jack-O'-Lantern out on the front porch or in the front window. Without a pumpkin, October would simply be another day, like April Thirteenth or September Tenth.

It was an outrage!

It was wrong!

It was…

A single word hit Henry's mind like an electric shock.

Blair.

CHAPTER EIGHT

As the sun rose on a new day, Henry lay in his bed knowing full well it was a Sunday but had no intention of going to church. He planned to stay in bed in protest. There was no way he would sit and watch Blair talk about the pumpkins. How dare he use his power to stop the pumpkin crop. How dare he!

From his bed, Henry could see his best Sunday clothes on the chair, where his mother had placed them the previous night. He could almost feel the itchiness from where he lay. Henry's mood was sour, and he couldn't think of anything that would cheer him up. Reverend Blair was insane if he thought he could ban Halloween.

Hearing the usual Sunday movements outside his door, Henry knew it was his mother waking his father.

A knock on the door.

"Come on Henry, it's church time," Carol called.

Henry folded his arm stubbornly. "I ain't going!"

The footsteps outside the door stopped. The door then flew open and Henry could see his mother in her best Sunday clothes; a yellow knee length dress and a big hat with a flower.

"Pardon?" she asked.

"I ain't going to church!"

"And why not, young man?"

"Blair wants to cancel Halloween," Henry stood his ground.

"That may be the case, but you are certainly going to church," Carol said with a firm voice. "Now get dressed in your suit and come downstairs."

Henry groaned and hid his head under the duvet. He thought of yesterday, when he and Maya had cycled back from Farmer Brown's place. How there would be no pumpkins this year. If Blair had reached out to the farmland, what else could he reach to? Mr. Raimi? Surely not. Mr. Raimi was a magician and therefore didn't fall under Blair's spell… but what about the other adults.

Below his bedroom, Henry heard the knock at the door followed by the murmurs of greetings.

"Come on Henry, the Foxes are here!" Carol called up the stairs.

The church was cold despite it being late

spring and the pews seemed even harder. Henry was right about the itchy suit and sat between his mother and Maya quietly scratching his legs. The congregation sat shivering in their pews as Blair, wearing his usual black robes, stepped up to the pulpit and held out a hand for silence.

The church fell under his spell, but not Henry.

"Welcome all, on this crisp May morning. We must thank the Lord for such a beautiful day. As many of you may be aware, the farmland surrounding our little town has been sown and fresh plants and vegetables have been planted. We thank those farmers for their hard work. But what you might not know is that there is one plant that has not been planted this year," Blair paused, as if waiting for a reaction but was only met with silence. "Pumpkins. The good Farmer Brown came to me with a trouble and I set his mind at ease. Some of you may remember my service back in November, which may seem like a lifetime ago for some of you. You are all aware of my feelings towards this Halloween. The Devil's night. A night where we allow our children to celebrate a day that glorifies demons, monsters and ghouls. We allow our OWN children to dress up as vile things and think that it's okay. I can assure you, it is NOT."

Henry was getting angry and judging by the way Maya was clenching her fists, he could tell she was mad too.

Blair continued, both hands gripping the pulpit. "This so-called tradition has gone on for too long! It's blasphemous and against our Lord. We can no longer allow such a thing to happen again. Every time we're, or should I say you are, letting your children dress up and go door to door begging for their sweets, you are directly angering the Lord and he does not stand for it. I have seen the holy way and the way is to ban Halloween."

Henry's fingernails dug so deep into his hands as he clenched his fists that he worried they would puncture the skin and draw blood. He didn't care. His anger burned under his skin.

"Over the past few months, I have been talking with the good town folk about their opinions and found most of you, excluding a select few bad eggs… (Henry knew Blair was looking for Grandpa Ray and Mr. Raimi) …most of the town folks here, the good, God fearing, townsfolk want us to rid ourselves of this Halloween once and for all."

Blair gestured to the front row of pews and people began to stand. First there was Farmer Brown, looking unusual in a neat suit rather than his usual grey jumpsuit. Next followed Mayor Proctor, a tall man with a hooked nose and wearing an expensive looking green suit.

Following him, was Mary Proctor, his wife. Susan Holtz, the town council leader, then Robert Red, the school supervisor.

"These fine people have joined me in the effort to rid the town of Halloween. Mr. Charles Brown, a good and decent man, has decided he shall not plant pumpkins this year but instead will plant luscious corn for us all. Mayor Proctor, my dear and loyal friend, has backed me and signed a new piece of legislation forbidding ALL stores in town from stocking any Halloween supplies or decorations and Mr. Robert Red has already joined the cause while Susan Holtz has backed the legislation," Blair listed.

The rage boiled within Henry and he could see his Grandpa Ray was just as mad.

"Now, you can see our leaders are deciding to do the right thing and I ask upon all of you to do the same. I propose a vote from all the good people of this beloved town of mine. I ask upon you now, to raise a hand if you want our town to be free from the vile Halloween," Blair went silent and looked over the church.

Henry held his breath, unable to believe such a thing had been proposed… but then the first hand went up… then another… then another… and another. Soon, nearly all the hands in front of him had been raised into the air. Looking behind him, Henry could see the sea of raised hands, all the church had raised their hands… and in the parting, could see Mr. Raimi shake his head.

Henry could feel tears well in his eyes. He felt helpless and wanted to stand up for his precious Halloween, but knew his crying would solve nothing.

Blair slammed his big hand down on the pulpit. "There we have it. You have all done that right thing. The decent thing. Halloween 1993 is cancelled!"

Without realizing he was doing it, Henry sprung to his feet. "No! You can't!"

Carol quickly pulled her son back down to the pews, but Henry knew the twisted smile on Blair's face was the most wicked he had ever seen.

CHAPTER NINE

After church, Henry knocked on every door of every kid he knew. He was going to need all the help he could get this time. Maya trailed behind, telling each new kid where they were headed. The Den.

The Den was hidden away in the woods surrounding the castle ruins and to an uneducated adult it was simply a clearing in the woods, tucked away under the low branches of the hanging trees. The children of course knew better. It was THEIR place and they could play games, read comic books, and pretty much do what they liked away from the prying eyes of the grown-ups. The children had made it their own. They moved fallen trees to make benches and dug a pit in the middle where they could make a bonfire when the light drained from the skies in the Autumn months. The usual residents of The Den were Henry, Maya, Zimmy and Jim Hall and they could be found there any given afternoon after school… if the adults looked properly.

It was a safe haven.

A secure place.

A wonderful secret.

And now, sitting on the logs, were eight kids. They all sat quietly and stared at Henry and Maya who stood before them.

Henry waited for the nerves to settle within him before speaking. "We all know why we're here…"

"I don't," said Charlotte May.

"No, me neither," said Zimmy, taking a bite out of an apple.

Maya stepped forward. "We're here because of what Blair said, he wants…"

The group of kids began to mutter among themselves, from a quiet whisper to loud talking.

Henry looked to the side and saw Kelly Krug and Tobe Green had turned up too and were waiting to hear Henry speak. If he didn't soon, no kid would be safe from punches and from Kelly and Tobe. It was a delicate situation.

"We're here because Reverend Blair wants to ban Halloween and we can't let him!" said Henry trying to sound firm.

"And what do you think you'll do about it huh?" Kelly called out, making a few kids flinch.

The question stumped Henry. He was so angry over Blair's ridiculous plan that he never stopped to think what he might actually do about it.

"That's why I have gathered you all here. No one here wants there to be no Halloween, do they?" asked Henry.

The small sea of faces all groaned and shook their heads.

"We all love Halloween and I'll be damned if I'm doing nothing to stop Blair. Why, imagine a year with no costumes or pumpkins or trick or treating. Can you imagine such a thing?"

Zimmy stood and threw his apple core aside. "I don't see what the guy's problem is. My rabbi never says anything about Halloween. Why has this Blair got such a problem?"

The children concurred in unison.

Henry was lost for an answer. "I don't know. Maybe he's just mean and doesn't like seeing kids have fun. Maybe he's just that mean. Do we need to know his 'why?' All we need to know is that this morning at church he took a vote and all the adults agreed to ban it. Heck, even most of our parents were right behind him. They were nodding and agreeing with everything he said."

"Maybe they put something in that holy water," chuckled Zimmy.

The children giggled.

"It doesn't matter why," Henry began, feeling brave. "None of the whys matter. He's banning it so what are all of us going to do?"

The children murmured amongst themselves.

"We're only kids, what can we do?" Charlotte May said, digging a shoe into the mud.

Again, Henry hadn't thought that far ahead.

Maya turned to her neighbour looking for answers.

Henry thought for a moment and remembered his Grandpa Ray. "I made a promise to my grandpa that I wouldn't let Halloween die and I'm not letting him down. We all need to, you know, band together."

"Why should we help you nerds?" asked Tobe Green.

Henry was nervous.

Maya took Henry's hand. It gave him a stillness and strength.

"Because…" Henry kept his voice steady and strong. "Because we all want the same thing. We all want our Halloween. The more kids we have, the better we'll do. Whatever plan we come up with…I want to call for a truce."

Tobe scoffed. "A truce? A truce to what?"

Henry stepped closer to the bully. "A truce that you won't pick on any of us until after Halloween. If you help us till then… then you can pick on us all you want."

His palms were sweaty with nerves. Never

before had Henry spoken so directly to a bully.

"And what if we don't?" asked Kelly, stepping up to the front, shoving two kids out the way.

"You want Halloween too," Henry said bravely.

He hoped it was the right response.

The two bullies looked at each other and seemed to turn the idea of a truce over in their minds.

Tobe grinned a mischievous grin.

"Okay Crane, you got a deal. We hear-by agree to not bully until dawn on November First,1993." he said. "A spit oath to make it official."

Tobe snorted and spat thick phlegm into the palm of his hand and held it toward Henry, who spat down into his own hand and after a moment of mistrust and hesitation, shook Tobe's hand.

"Deal," said Henry.

"Deal," said Tobe.

The hushed whispers of the children quietened as they watched something amazing happen. A truce between kid and bully alike. A spit oath, as they all knew, was unbreakable.

Jim Hall stood up, bursting with enthusiasm "We need a name. A name for our crusade against Blair."

Maya thought for just a second and welled her

chest. "We'll call ourselves 'The Midnight Pumpkin Society'."

And all the children, kid and bully alike, agreed.

CHAPTER TEN

Dinner was over and as his parents cleared the table, Henry sat with Grandpa Ray in silence. The meeting at The Den was still fresh in Henry's mind and he could barely contain the drive and motivation to start their little rebellion. He was bursting with possibilities.

Grandpa Ray, being a wise magician, must have sensed Henry's excitement.

"Penny for your thoughts, Henry," he asked, stirring his coffee with a pen from his shirt pocket.

Henry looked past his grandpa to make sure his parents were busy in the kitchen and out of ear shot before he spoke. "We started a group."

Grandpa Ray leant closer, his interest peaked. "What kind of group?"

"We're going to stop Blair and save Halloween."

A smile spread across Grandpa Ray's face. It was warm and kind. "Well look at you. And how will you do it?"

"He'll never know what we're up to. We've got a hiding place… it's down by…"

Grandpa Ray held up a hand and shook his head. "If I don't know then no one can get the answer out of me. You keep it secret."

Henry understood and nodded, tapping his nose with his finger.

Grandpa Ray winked. "If there is anything I can help with, you only have to ask. You're such a wonderful grandson."

"I can't break my promise," Henry said dutifully.

"Well you won't I'm sure. If you stick to your guns and set your mind to it, I'm sure you can accomplish many great things Henry."

Henry tried to visualize the plan to save Halloween in his mind but realized that he didn't have one. October was just about five months away, which may seem a long time to some but seemed like next week to Henry. He began to turn ideas over in his head.

"How many other adults have you told?" Grandpa Ray asked, sipping his coffee between words.

Henry shook his head. "No adults, except you."

With a wave of his finger, Grandpa Ray

winked. "You know who I think would be a worthy friend in your battle?"

"Who?"

"Mr. Raimi."

Henry thought. Grandpa Ray wouldn't just suggest someone who would stop their plan. If Grandpa Ray said Mr. Raimi could be trusted, then he most certainly could.

"I think tomorrow you should go talk to Mr. Raimi and see if he'll join your cause. I think he just might," Grandpa Ray said with a pat on Henry's shoulder.

Henry sat quietly, thinking how horrid Blair had sounded in church and how Mr. Raimi had walked out. He knew Mr. Raimi was a devotee of Halloween and Mr. Raimi wasn't like the other adults. He sat and listened, just like Grandpa Ray did. When telling Mr. Raimi a story after school while picking up evening sweets, he'd listen to your whole story as if you were the only kid in town, never interrupting or telling you to be quiet, but he listened and laughed right along with you.

Henry looked at the grandfather clock in the hallway, just beyond the dining room archway. "What time does Mr. Raimi's store close?"

Henry looked up at Mr. Raimi with hopeful eyes. He had just told him of the secret Midnight

Pumpkin Society and their plan, and just like before, Mr. Raimi had stood quietly and listened to the whole story, only pausing to serve the last customers buying a bottle of milk."

"So… that's what we're going to do," Henry said finally, sticking his hands in his pockets.

Mr. Raimi stood quietly, a curious look on his face. "You think you can pull it off?"

Henry nodded.

"And you think none of the adults would help you except me and your Grandpa Ray?"

"Nope. They're all agreeing with Blair."

Mr. Raimi nodded reluctantly, no doubt hating to acknowledge the truth.

"I know you want Halloween just as much as we do, Mr. Raimi. I saw it on your face when you walked out of church. You felt exactly what the rest of us kids felt," Henry said, stepping up to the counter.

Mr. Raimi grinned. "I *do* love Halloween that is a fact… and I sure don't want to see Blair win this one. But you know I'm not allowed to stock any Halloween items this year? Nor can I sell pumpkins or costumes. Not even orange and black streamers."

"I know. We'll think of something… but we need an adult… I don't know… to listen out for us."

"You mean like a secret spy?" Mr. Raimi chuckled.

"Exactly! Someone who can tell us if anyone suspects anything or have caught onto our plan," Henry explained.

Mr. Raimi rubbed his bearded chin, but Henry knew what the answer would be by the mischievous smile on the shopkeeper's face.

"You've got yourself a deal, Mr. Crane," Mr. Raimi held out his big hand, which Henry shook firmly.

Taking a pouch of pipe tobacco from the shelf behind him, Mr. Raimi pushed it across the counter toward Henry. "Now, take this to your grandpa and tell him I'm in."

Henry bolted from the shop and ran down the street full of delight and happiness knowing they had someone in their corner to help the fight.

CHAPTER ELEVEN

Maya sat on her front porch with the old typewriter in front of her as she gently tapped out a letter she'd give to all the Midnight Pumpkin Society. It was their duty to save Halloween and slowly, over the last two weeks, ideas had come trickling in. Zimmy, who didn't know Blair or go to the same type of church as the rest of the kids, had come up with the most ideas with Henry close behind. The other kids had been popping with ideas and inspiration, but they were yet to set their plan in motion. Maybe it was the looming summer, a fatal distraction from the plan, or maybe it was simply the other kids had lost interest. Maya tried to deny the latter but felt deep down that it might be the case.

As Maya looked up, stopping her two-finger typing, she saw a shy little girl standing at the bottom of the porch steps. It took Maya a moment to recognize the girl for she was rarely seen.

It was Elizabeth Blair. The reverend's daughter.

She wore her neat brown hair in curls that surrounded her face and wore tidy clothes, not grass stained on the knees like Maya's jeans. Elizabeth wore the type of clothes most kids only wore on a Sunday. Prim and proper.

Maya stood but Elizabeth spoke first.

"I know what you're doing," she said.

Maya felt her heart skip a beat. "I don't know what you mean."

Elizabeth took a step up to the porch. "You're going to try and save Halloween, to stop my dad."

Maya remembered what Henry had told her after the last meeting at The Den. Don't tell anyone else about the Midnight Pumpkin Society, especially someone so close to Blair.

Maya simply shook her head.

"But…" Elizabeth stepped onto the porch and looked at Maya, who was another step closer to going inside the house. "I want to help you."

Stopping mid-step, Maya wondered if she had heard correctly.

"I want to help you," Elizabeth repeated.

Maya was suspicious. "Why?"

"So, you *are* trying to stop my dad?"

"I didn't say that. Why would you help if we were?" Maya asked, crossing her arms. She had to tread carefully.

"I… I like Halloween too."

"How can the daughter of Reverend Blair like Halloween?" Maya said with disbelief.

"I used to celebrate it with my mother…before she died. She used to carve pumpkins with me and take me trick or treating. But since she died, my dad seems to hate Halloween. She died on Halloween. Since then he's wanted to get rid of Halloween. He wants to get rid of all those wonderful things," Elizabeth explained. "It's sad, really."

Maya didn't let her guard down but felt sad at the thought of losing a mum.

"I guess… well maybe he's upset with Halloween… But I don't want it to go, it reminds me too much of my mother. I really want to help you," continued Elizabeth.

It felt like a trap to Maya. Had Blair put his own daughter up to this? Did Blair already know about the society?

"Please. Let me help you," Elizabeth's eyes were, it seemed, truthful and honest.

After a long moment of thought, Maya said, "Meet me at the castle at dusk. Don't tell anyone."

Under the shade of the giant oak tree that hung over the castle's entrance, Henry, Maya, Zimmy, Dylan Samuel and Hunter Tapert stood with their bikes and waited for Elizabeth to show. Each child had their reservations and they had come to an agreed test for Elizabeth after much discussion.

Night was creeping closer. Lurking shadows emerged from all directions.

"Do you think she's backed out?" asked Hunter, after a few quiet minutes.

They all looked to Maya.

"I don't think so… she said she'd be here. She looked dead serious when she asked to help," Maya explained.

Zimmy waved a hand. "Why, that could just be her nervous to ask because she knows that we think she's in cahoots with her dad."

"No… I don't think so. The way she talked about it…" Maya said, thinking back to the front porch meeting.

The girl seemed genuine, but it was hard to be sure.

"We'll wait another ten minutes," Henry said.

And so, they waited, with the wind picking up and the shadows nipping at their heels.

With just a minute left, Elizabeth came jogging around the corner. She huffed and puffed as if she were running a marathon.

Hunter stepped forward. "We didn't think

you'd show up."

"I'm sorry. My dad was asking where I was going," said Elizabeth, catching her breath.

"What did you tell him?" asked Henry.

"I said I was going to borrow a book from a friend a few streets ago, so I don't have long."

"Come on. We don't have long," Henry said, eyeing the sunset.

They dropped their bikes to the floor and walked through the castle entrance into the inner lush green courtyard where they could see Blair's church standing empty and quiet. Creepy and mean.

Henry pointed to the small church and looked at Elizabeth. "We want you to toilet paper Blair's car. It's parked just by the church."

Elizabeth looked shocked. "What?!"

Dylan stepped closer. "You heard. He said you need to T.P your dad's car. We need know whose side you're on."

Maya stayed quiet, uncomfortable with the peer pressure they were putting on the poor girl.

"If I do it… you'll let me help you?" Elizabeth asked, taking the bulging backpack Henry held out for her.

"Yes. Call it an initiation, I guess. We need to know we can trust you," said Henry.

Elizabeth held the toilet paper in her hand and looked at her father's car parked carefully under a tree. She took a few intrepid steps closer. Over her shoulder, the others watched with crossed arms and silent faces.

And then like a wind-up toy springing to life, Elizabeth jumped and ran to the car, pulling a roll of toilet paper from the bag and hurling it high and far. The roll hit the roof and rolled down the other side. Again and again, Elizabeth threw the toilet paper in arcs, falling and rising until the car was almost completely covered.

Maya, Henry, Hunter, Dylan and Zimmy watched in disbelief. They knew then that they could trust her. The children could hardly contain their glee at the thought of Blair discovering the car the next day. It was a sweet treat to think of Blair's anger.

He deserved it.

When Elizabeth returned with the empty backpack, the society all shook her hand and gave her a wink and a smile.

She was accepted.

They all ran and cycled down Castle Street just as the streetlights burst to life.

CHAPTER TWELVE

Just as Henry had hoped, Blair was furious over the toilet paper incident and spoke in church about it, urging the perpetrator to come forward and take their punishment but no one did and he was unaware of the stifled giggles of Henry, Maya, Hunter and Elizabeth in the pews. As Blair spoke more about his plan for October Thirty-First, Henry couldn't help but feel a strong sensation of anger and excitement. He thought of the society's plan and he knew he would show Blair that the children of Port Hampton wouldn't take it. They would show all the grown-ups that Halloween lived forever and they couldn't simply repress it

As they left church, stripping off their smart ties and ruffling up their hair, they could tell that May had become June. It was warmer and the wind was pleasant on their faces. It was very nearly time to leave school and enjoy the whole summer ahead of them. While the adults assumed the children would be out playing stick in the mud and hide and seek innocently, they would, in fact, begin their plan.

A little after One P.M., after lunch, the town's children all slunk away to The Den, away from prying adult eyes.

Henry and Maya stood before the rest of the kids. They all dropped their voices and waited. Even Kelly Krug and Tobe Green were quiet.

"As you know, we're now in June. We have a week left of school and then we need to start work…" Henry's voice gave a squeak on the last word and the other children giggled.

He coughed and tried to hide it. "We have one week left of school and I think we need to use it to our advantage."

"How?" asked Charlotte May.

Henry tried to speak but found no words came.

The children began whispering loudly.

"Hey now," Maya stepped forward, clutching a book under her arm. "Now look here, we might not have all the details right now, but this book will sure help us."

She held it up for all to see. A bright coloured book with bats, spiders and a Jack-O'-Lantern on the front.

Hunter squinted over his glasses and read the title out loud. "*Make your own Halloween.*"

Excited whispers grew louder.

"Where did you get that?" asked Kelly, while chewing on a chocolate bar.

"The library," Maya said, trying to keep her fear of Kelly hidden. "Well, Henry's Grandpa Ray ordered it in for us."

"He wants to help us…but he's old," Henry explained.

"Is he gonna help us make all this stuff?" asked Hunter, looking over the book cover.

"Well, he wants to see us fight our own battles. He said the best victories are the ones we earn. The ones we really fight for," Henry tried to sound strong and like a leader, for he knew in his heart of hearts they were fighting a worthy cause. "This book tells you how to make your own Halloween decorations and they're all made from household stuff. Things we can still get even though there's the ban; bin liners, toilet paper, papier-mâché, spray paint, stuff like that."

"I see," Hunter smiled.

"We can gather supplies from school," Zimmy chimed in.

"Exactly," replied Henry. "Me and Maya have looked over the Halloween book and made a list of everything we need and some of it can be found in the art room at school. If we can distract Miss. Bennett, one of us can sneak into the supply cupboard and fill our bags. It's a bit naughty but this is for Halloween, guys."

"If we all break into different groups and tackle one thing, we could make enough decorations to cover whatever we need," Henry said.

"How much are we covering anyways?" Jim Hall asked, standing up.

Henry was lost for an answer, he hadn't thought that far ahead. Just decorating their bedrooms wouldn't mean a thing. The decorations had to be seen by all.

Then suddenly, the idea hit him like electricity.

Henry smiled as his thoughts came together. "We'll decorate the whole town."

Jim waved a hand. "Ah, now you're talking crazy!"

"Am I?" Henry said, walking into the middle of the group. "Look, how many of us are there? Why, if we broke up into smaller groups, each taking a different street or two we could cover the town in no time at all."

"I agree with Henry," Maya yelled.

"Mayor Proctor has banned all shops from selling Halloween things in town, so we won't have any help there. We're on our own. If we treat this book like our bible then we can't be stopped," explained Henry.

"We'll need to hide the stuff somewhere," said Dylan Samuel, kicking at the dirt at his feet.

Henry thought.

Maya thought.

There were obstacles in their way. The plan might have seemed so clear in their minds but once they actually began to think about it and plan, it seemed much weaker than first thought.

"Why not keep the stuff here?" Jim suggested. "Here at the Den."

"Yeah, my mum said we're in for a drought this summer so there won't be any rain. Would that work?" asked Alex Thorne, chewing his gum.

"I think so, yeah," Henry said.

"Then what are we waiting for?" Maya asked, jumping to her feet.

CHAPTER THIRTEEN

And so, summer began. School, with its boring math classes and dreary history lessons, broke out at the end of June and the whole warm season was ahead of the children of Port Hampton. With education put to sleep for nearly six weeks, the children could focus on their duties to the Midnight Pumpkin Society, something that had sat in all their excited minds during the last few weeks of school. It was a duty they spoke of in hushed whispers behind hands and into each other's ears. Not that the adults had any idea about what they were planning (except Grandpa Ray and Mr. Raimi). The children had done well to keep their secret and not a single kid had blabbed or mentioned a word.

Every child had their job, and every child took to their job with glee and wonderful mischief.

A borrowed bedsheet from someone's parent's unguarded clothesline. A few art supplies from the school cupboard (unnoticed by Miss Bennett). Mr. Raimi searched his stockroom and provided old tins of orange and black paint and sheets of plywood. Grandpa Ray told the society all about the decorations he had made as a child and showed them how to make them. Jim Hall began making tubs of papier-mâché from old newspapers he had collected from the neighbourhood. Hunter Tapert dived into dusty and cobwebbed attic trunks and boxes looking for past Halloween goodies. Kelly Krug turned out to be quite the painter and was busy working on a mini Halloween masterpiece. Tobe Green took to borrowing shirts and trousers from his dad's cupboard with a clear idea about how to use them. Charlotte May was excellent at sewing and took to her job with great enthusiasm. Maya Fox spent hours cutting orange velvet and black felt while Henry Crane began designing and making the most important parts; the masks and the Jack-O'-Lanterns.

Slowly, as summer leaves turned from golden green to yellow then deep red, the Den became a stockpile of their handmade decorations and festive goodies. Every kid brought their sleepover tents and Dylan Samuel even provided a big camouflage bedsheet he had found at a thrift store in Crowthrone.

It all fitted perfectly and was well hidden from the adults prying eyes.

The plan was coming together.

Henry watched a maroon leaf fall from the tree above. It drifted down in the gentle breeze and came to a rest upon his shoe.

Autumn was truly here at last.

Looking over the kids in front of him, Henry knew he had a group of loyal friends and he had even begun to feel like Kelly Krug and Tobe Green might be his friend. Every kid had been dedicated and had never lost their passion and drive for saving their most important day.

"We're nearly ready," Henry began. "Tomorrow is October First and that just gives us thirty days until the big day and we're so close to being ready."

"You've all done great! Just look at all the stuff we've done!" Maya pointed with pride at the four pop up tents filled with their homemade creations and macabre props. "We're really gonna make Blair mad with all this!"

The society cheered and Dylan Samuel started a round of applause.

"It's true, we have made a lot of progress, but we can still get caught so we need to keep our mouths shut and not say a work to any grown up. Especially not your dad, Elizabeth," said Henry.

Elizabeth crossed her heart with her finger and smiled. "Never. Scout's honour."

"Good," Henry nodded. "As long as we keep hush, Blair will never catch on. Or any of the adults if we do our job right."

"Each one of us had done great. Give

yourselves a pat on the back," smiled Maya, standing next to Henry like a loyal solider. "We're gonna sneak up on Blair and he'll never see us coming. I can almost taste those Halloween treats."

The Midnight Pumpkin Society cheered.

They were close.

CHAPTER FOURTEEN

Henry's parents had gone to the Scala Cinema as they did almost every Saturday night, leaving Henry alone with Grandpa Ray and it wasn't long before Grandfather and Grandson were talking about The Midnight Pumpkin Society.

"It sounds like you have it nearly ready," said Grandpa Ray, pouring his special coffee with a dash of brandy.

"We're gonna do it, Grandpa. I promise." Henry was sure of this.

Grandpa Ray sat down in his armchair with a sigh. It reminded Henry that his grandfather was old, which always seemed hard to believe as Grandpa Ray had the youth, enthusiasm, and wit of a thousand rosy cheeked boys.

"I can't wait for you to smack the nonsense from Blair's mouth, Henry. I really can't. The man is a nut and I can't believe what he's trying to do."

"Grandpa, why do you love Halloween so much?" Henry asked, sitting down at his grandfather's feet.

"Oh my, such a question," Grandpa Ray beamed. "I'm in love with a mistress and her name is All Hallows Eve. The spookiest of nights where electricity bounces from one kid to another. A night where you can become, just for that one special night, anything you can imagine; a spider, witch, monster, ghoul, werewolf, or vampire. The possibilities are endless. Why, we scare each other Halloween night to remind us that we're alive! And what better night to be alive than Halloween night. It charges our bones, flesh, and mind. It lets us live out our fantasies and run free and wild.

"Halloween is about honouring the dead and keeping their memories alive. Spirits walk the earth on Halloween night, when the border between the lands of the living and the dead is at its thinnest. We wear gruesome masks to protect us from the bad wandering spirits and to keep us safe, allowing us to blend in with the phantoms of yesteryear, long gone but not forgotten.

"The wind feels different on October thirty-first, don't you think? It's intoxicating. It whispers with the calls of a thousand lost souls and chills you to your core. It never feels like that at Christmas or Easter, does it? No, only on Halloween. The night sky is a deeper black than any other night. It's a void into the wonderful and macabre. The smell of pumpkin innards and of pumpkin pies baking lifts me off my feet like something from a *Tom & Jerry* cartoon. You don't smell those wonderful smells any other time of year.

"All these things fit just perfectly, like a tight puzzle, on October thirty-first. All Hallows Eve, Samhain, Halloween! We've got to save it, Henry. For what would October and autumn be without that most special of nights? You have the power, Henry. You and Maya and all your young friends. I would be very sad that if in my last remaining years, I would miss out on just one single Halloween…"

Grandpa Ray sighed, looking down into his coffee mug.

Henry stood and embraced his grandfather with all his might. "I'll save it. It'll be the best Halloween you ever saw. I promise."

A tear rolled down the elderly man's face and he wept with joy.

As did Henry

CHAPTER FIFTEEN

The sun rose differently on October first, 1993.

It glowed a different way that appeared at no other time during the year. Something about it stirred young Henry Crane, who watched from his window as the sun climbed up over the horizon. Within him, he could feel satisfaction and excitement for he knew they were close to accomplishing their goal. Everything had gone to plan so far and there was just thirty more days to get things finished. He was proud of himself, proud that he had united the children of the town. He had brought them together and there was no longer such a thing as a bully. All kids were there to help each other and save Halloween. It almost felt like having your cake and eating it too.

And now, as crisp autumn leaves danced in the breeze and drifted to the ground, Henry knew they would win. They had worked hard. The wait for Halloween to come was almost too much to contain and the sunrise gave Henry a calmness, a stillness to allow himself the simple pleasure of knowing it was now just a matter of time before they won. Though, as he thought more about it, Henry wondered just what would happen if they were caught. What would Blair do? What *could* Blair do? Make them read the bible cover to cover? Scrub the church floor? Clean the pipe organ? No doubt the adults would all agree with the punishment.

On more than one occasion Henry's parents had mentioned the cancelled Halloween and how it would be good for the kids of this town to go without it. Of course, Grandpa Ray was still outspoken, calling Blair a blowhard and not fit to lead. It was Grandpa Ray's stories of Halloween as a child that kept Henry hopeful and motivated. When doubt entered Henry's mind, he had only to turn to his loyal grandfather.

Once the sun was over the roofs of the surrounding houses, Henry dressed and went downstairs filled with the energy of a thousand suns.

Grandpa Ray sat at the kitchen table with his coffee and toast. He looked up from his morning newspaper and winked. "Going to The Den, young Henry?"

"Maya is meeting me there," Henry said, pulling on his parka coat.

"What's on today's agenda?"

"She thinks she may have found a better way

to make Jack-O'-Lanterns."

"Good! You can't do Halloween without them," Grandpa Ray dropped a warm hand onto his grandson's shoulder and smiled. "You're doing it. You're really doing it!"

The glint in his grandfather's eye warmed Henry and made him feel secure.

Pedalling away down Castle Street on his bike in the mild weather, Henry couldn't help but feel happy. It was like that Christmas feeling, knowing that there was a surprise you wanted to share but had to wait until just the right moment. The wind, now special as it was indeed October, ran through his hair and over his hands.

Today was the start of something great.

As he turned his bike down into the alley leading to the castle ruins, he could hear a sound.

It was a sound he couldn't quite place at first. He looked through his memory for such a sound, but it took him a little while to process it.

The breaking of wood, the roar of a chainsaw, digging shovels and men talking.

The sound was coming…from The Den.

Henry skidded to a halt and looked through the bushes toward The Den.

The once heavily wooded area was a shell of its former self. It was close to being unrecognizable and Henry was, for a moment, unsure he had come the right way. Gone were the overhanging branches and the clearing in the heavy woods was now fully exposed. A group of men with shovels, pickaxes, rakes, shears, and wheelbarrows were digging out the very earth of The Den.

The Den had been destroyed.

It was gone.

And standing, looking on, was Blair.

CHAPTER SIXTEEN

They had lost. Blair had won and there was nothing they could do about it.

Henry stood rooted to the spot with a sinking feeling deep in his stomach. He suspected Blair was aware that he had just seen The Den destroyed and that Blair took pleasure knowing one of the children was watching. Henry could see the smug look on Blair's face.

The plan had failed, all their hard work burnt and destroyed before Henry's very eyes. How he wanted to curse Blair for his wicked meanness.

It took Henry what felt like an hour to turn away from what was once their precious and secure Den and mount his bike and head back up Castle Street. Every hard pedal felt like salt in the wounds. He wanted to cry but didn't want to give Blair the satisfaction. The reverend deserved not a single tear! To Henry, it felt like the mild autumn day had now turned into a vicious rainstorm and had washed away his hopes and dreams. All was gone thanks to Blair's vile hand.

As Henry slowly pedalled around the corner of

Proctor Street, he could see Maya waiting on her front porch. She jumped up and ran down the path toward him.

"They've destroyed it!" she cried, waving her hands above her head.

"Blair was there," Henry said, defeated. "We're sunk."

A big smile spread across Maya's face.

"What?" asked Henry, dropping his bike to the floor.

"I got there first," she smiled, full of mischief.

Maya's bedroom, which was messy at best to begin with, was now a room dedicated to All Hallows Eve. On every possible surface and shelf were the society's decorations and ghoulish treats; bedsheet ghosts, papier-mâché Jack-O'-Lanterns and bats, cans of orange and black paint, streamers, balloons, cardboard skeletons, cotton thread cobwebs, bags of candy and delicious apples to caramelize. All the wonders of Halloween were before them, saved and safe. The happiness welled in Henry's chest like a big balloon. His spirits were lifted to a place he never thought he could have reached less than an hour ago.

"How did you save so much?"

Maya looked down at her feet. "I have to confess… I had to… I had to tell an adult."

"What?!" Henry panicked.

Maya nervously clapped her hands together. "I had to tell my mum, I needed her help moving everything…she wants to help us."

At that moment, Dawn Fox came into the room with a tatty brown cardboard box in her arms. There were plastic bones sticking out of the top. Relics of past Halloweens.

"'Here we go dear, Mr. Raimi said this was all he had left in the stockroom. Stuff he didn't sell last year," Dawn said, putting down the box. "Hiya Henry!"

Henry didn't know what to say. Though he loved Dawn Fox like he did his own mother, he was mistrustful, wondering if she would tell the other adults about the Midnight Pumpkin Society.

Dawn smiled at her young neighbour. "Henry, I've been talking to Sam…I mean, Mr. Raimi and he told me all about your little club, as did your Grandpa Ray and although at first I must say I was taken aback by what they told me…"

Henry stiffened. This was it. They would be exposed and punished.

"I can promise you, your secret is safe with me. I shan't say a word," Dawn said with a wink. "I also suspect you now need a new home base."

"Yeah, Blair, he broke The Den up…" Henry sighed and sat on the bed.

"Well I think the Fox house would make a perfect place, don't you?" Maya said to her mother, wrapping her small arms around her.

"So do I," said Dawn.

Henry could barely contain his glee. All was not lost. They could still save Halloween.

He was turning over the society's plan in his head, feeling confident knowing they had saved all their hard work, when a question entered his mind, and it was a question he needed an answer to. It was too important not to share.

"How do you think Blair found out about The Den?" he asked Maya.

Maya folded her arms. "I think we both know. I had doubts about her when she first walked onto the porch. Elizabeth Blair snitched to her dad."

Maya's face turned red and Henry agreed.

There was a rat in the Midnight Pumpkin Society.

CHAPTER SEVENTEEN

With great gusto, the children of the Midnight Pumpkin Society took to recreating and refining their spooky decorations, creepy costumes, and gruesome mementos ready for the last day of the month. Every idea was fantastic and wonderful. No kid was called stupid for bringing something new to the table and no kid was left with nothing to do. The work they were doing at the Fox house made their first attempts at The Den look amateur.

They were back and no one, not even mean-spirited Blair, would be able to stop them now. Halloween would never die, not while Henry and Maya had breath in their lungs.

But, as much as they were excited for their fantastic plan and ideas, there was still a problem. They had to confront the rat in the society.

Henry cycled around the neighbourhood and gathered all the members of the society and brought them back to the Fox house, where they made themselves into a circle in the back garden.

There were murmurs around the circle of kids as they sat in the sweet October warmth with the gentle rustle of wind around them.

Henry stood before the circle and waited for silence.

"As you all know," Henry began. "Blair got to The Den. He ripped it all up and we never saw him coming. Just another obstacle in our way but we're strong enough to beat him and we will, believe me. But something has happened…Blair must have found out about The Den from one of us so that means we have a rat in the society. Someone blabbed to old man Blair and they have risked exposing our whole plan."

Henry felt like an army sergeant addressing his troops. His loyal army.

There were shouts and cries from every kid, each furious and hysterical with fingers pointing in every direction. Each kid turning to their neighbour and accusing them of being the rat.

"Hey! Hey!" Maya called, trying for silence. "We know who the rat is."

"Who?" asked one of the kids.

"Yeah, who is it?" another kid asked.

Maya took a deep breath. She hated confrontation and felt mean for what she was about to say but knew it had to be said out loud and they had to rid themselves of the snitch.

The society fell silent with anticipation.

"It's Elizabeth Blair! She told her dad about The Den," Maya pointed a finger at Elizabeth.

The girl began to cry. "No! It isn't me! I swear!"

The kids started shouting, some threw dead leaves at her.

"Who else would tell Blair about the Den? Huh? It was all fine before you came along," said Kelly Krug.

"I promise it's not me, I would never…" Elizabeth pleaded.

"We need to take a vote," said Henry.

Hunter stood. "Everyone who wants Elizabeth out, hold up your hands."

The kids all raised their hands in a wave, all of them staring at Elizabeth.

Henry couldn't help but feel for Elizabeth. He knew he couldn't tell for sure if it were indeed her, but she sure looked suspicious from where he stood.

"I'm sorry Elizabeth," Henry gulped. "You're banished from the Midnight Pumpkin Society."

All the children turned their backs on Elizabeth Blair who, with huge tears in her eyes, ran to the garden's side gate and out of view.

Henry could hear her tears running on the Autumn winds and he felt sad and full of shame.

CHAPTER EIGHTEEN

October 24th. A Sunday.

The church was, as usual, chilled like a morgue. There were hushed whispers as Blair stepped up to the pulpit. For once the fact that they were in church was irrelevant to Henry and Maya. They weren't irritated or bored for they sat barely able to contain their giggles as they thought of the society and their plan. They had spoken to Mr. Raimi and now he had his own part in their plan. It had been Mr. Raimi's idea to host a party for all the adults on Halloween night giving the kids free reign to decorate the whole town without adults to stop them and they had inducted him into the society as a confidant. Mr. Raimi supported the cause just as much as any kid did and he was as much a kid as them.

Today, there was something about Blair that made Henry feel a little uneasy.

The reverend was smiling.

"Good morning, my friends and welcome to another service," he said in a calm and even voice, very unlike his usual booming voice.

"Morning," replied the congregation (except Henry, Maya, Grandpa Ray, Dawn and Mr. Raimi).

"Today is a fine day, a fine day indeed. I hope you are all doing well and trust you are here for a dose of the good book. I'm always glad to see your faces."

He was being too nice, Henry thought. Something was very wrong.

"The weather has been beautiful and handed down to us by the Lord for us all to enjoy. Some of you may have noticed the new landscaped garden we completed as you came through the main entrance. A beautiful job paid for with your kind donations and approved by Mayor Proctor," said Blair.

Mayor Proctor waved from the front row and his wife giggled.

Henry felt sour about the new garden. A garden that was once their Den.

"We are thankful for this new space where we may sit, reflect and pray to the Lord, thanking him for simple pleasures." Blair paused and rapped his fingers on the pulpit, still wearing that smug smile.

The silence was strange. Henry turned to Maya who had the same worried look on her face. In a way only kids can do, they both knew what the other was thinking. Blair was building to something and it wouldn't be something good.

On the other hand, Blair didn't know the society had a new home base and were ready to hatch their plan.

"We all know," Blair began. "that Devil's day is almost upon us and we have all made good on our promise to rid ourselves of it. And we know that is the right thing to do. So, pat yourselves on the back for doing the Lord's work and we shall be rewarded.

"I have some good news. Mr. Raimi, a former outspoken member of our flock, has decided to join us in throwing a party for us all on the night of the Thirty-First."

A giddy yelp jumped from Henry's throat and he had to hold a hand over his mouth to keep in the laughter. It was too delicious.

"Henry!" Carol whispered and tapped him on the leg.

"Thank you," said Mr. Raimi once the applause had died down. "Next Sunday at the town hall at Seven P.M. All come along and we'll… enjoy the Lord and celebrate our good fortunes."

Henry could tell Mr. Raimi was wearing a smile just as plastic as Blair's.

Everything was falling into place.

"Why, I'll even look the other way if you have a drink or two," Blair laughed, and the congregation laughed too.

Blair's kindness put Henry on edge.

"So, as us adults will be celebrating, Mayor Proctor has some words for the children," Blair said.

Mayor Proctor stood and took Blair's space as the pulpit.

"Morning everyone, hope to see you all at the party next week and remember I'm always here to listen to any more ideas you have about our kind town. But for now, you children. As of tomorrow, for your own safety and well-being, I am enforcing a Six P.M curfew."

The words hit Henry like a sucker punch.

CHAPTER NINETEEN

They sat on the Fox's front porch listening to the mournful sound of falling leaves. Not even the October smells could lift their spirits.

Henry and Maya sat with tears in their eyes.

Maya tried to comfort her friend.

"It's okay… something will help us out…"

She didn't believe her own words.

"How will we save Halloween now?" Henry said through angry tears.

"We'll find a way."

"How? The party was to keep the adults away and now we can't leave our houses. We'll never be able to keep our promise."

Henry felt miserable and defeated. The heavy feeling in his chest wouldn't lift. They were sunk and there was nothing they could do to fix it.

All was lost. This was a huge obstacle in their way.

Out of the front door came Dawn and Mr.

Raimi, carrying glasses of lemonade for the children and wine for themselves. They sat down on the wicker chairs looking out onto the auburn lit street. There was silence for a moment.

"What will we do Mr. Raimi?" sighed Henry.

Mr. Raimi smiled. It was mischievous and youthful as ever. "Who says Blair has won?"

"What do you mean?" asked Maya, cocking her head.

"I think I know exactly what he means," Grandpa Ray came hobbling up the front path, leaning heavy on his cane with a glass of his usual whiskey in his free hand. He was wearing the same youthful smile as Mr. Raimi.

"It seems to me," he began. "Blair has no way of keeping this curfew if he's at the party. Why it would only take my word, or Dawn's or Sam's, saying that little Maya and Henry are tucked up in bed and at home…when in fact you're out doing the right thing. No, I'm not a liar… but what's a little white fib for the greater good?"

Henry's tears became tears of admiration. He loved his grandfather so much.

"I can't see a problem now, can you Maya?" asked Dawn, smiling down at her daughter.

Maya shook her head.

"I sure can't." Mr. Raimi said, taking Dawn's hand.

Grandpa Ray slowly sat on the steps and looked kindly at the children. "Now, I made you promise not to let Halloween die, and I intend to help you every step of the way. It's your right to celebrate whatever you want to. Don't let Blair push his views on you, just because he's a blowhard and thinks Halloween is wicked doesn't make it so. Halloween is a joy, a celebration. What joy there is dressing as anything you can imagine for one spooky night to frighten and delight and as long as I'm still walkin' and talkin', I'm never gonna let him win."

"Us neither," said Mr. Raimi, and then he winked.

Henry was saved.

The society was saved again.

The plan would go ahead.

Though now the stakes were higher.

CHAPTER TWENTY

I t finally came. October Thirty-First, 1993.

Sweeping October winds and darkness contrasting the joyful orange spirits. Halloween came in its full glory and splendour. To the adults it was simply another day but for the Midnight Pumpkin Society it was a thing of beauty and excitement.

And as the evening drew closer and the adults dressed in bowties & dinner jackets, high heels & pearls and left their houses for the party, the Midnight Pumpkin Society ran, skipped and jumped to the Fox house through the fallen crisp leaves and delicate October mist…

CHAPTER TWENTY-ONE

The town hall on the corner of White Hart Lane was alight and busy. All the adults followed through the door into the quaintly decorated hall which looked well put together, not a pumpkin or orange and black streamer in sight. It could have been an evening in May or June.

The adults all wore their best Sunday clothes and gathered for an evening of cocktails and good conversation.

Mr. Raimi greeted them as they arrived and directed them to the bar, which, thanks to Mayor Proctor, was, what the adults called, an 'open' bar. It was not long before every adult in the place clutched a drink in their hand. The food, mostly finger foods, was laid out neatly on a long table, all manners of sweet and savoury.

The buzz of boring grown up conversation began.

The Midnight Pumpkin Society waited patiently at the Fox house for word from Maya and Zimmy. It was Dawn's idea to bring Maya along, claiming she couldn't find a babysitter and Zimmy's parents flat out didn't trust him alone at home, so he was brought to the party. Even though it meant having to wear itchy Sunday best clothes, it hardly mattered for they knew it was for the greater good. They were there as spies. Maya was carrying a walkie talkie that Henry had from his uncle for his birthday. Now, the society would be able to keep an eye on the party as the night unfolded. Maya had a plan for Blair and had pre-packed her backpack ready for it.

"Nice to see you," Mr. Raimi greeted Mr. and Mrs. Krug. He smiled and showed them through the door.

Behind the Krugs came Reverend Blair, wearing a dark suit and a darker smile.

"Mr. Raimi," Blair said, not extending his hand.

"It's nice to see you, Reverend. Are you looking forward to tonight's festivities?" asked Mr. Raimi.

"I am, I think it is a good thing you've done."

"Well, I try."

Blair rubbed his stern chin. "You know Raimi, I had you pegged as an opponent not a friend…"

Mr. Raimi stayed cool as ever, slipping into pleasantries easily. "Well, I had time to think about it and I… I think you're right about this Halloween so why not do away with it and enjoy the evening."

Blair didn't answer and looked over the shopkeeper. "We shall see."

Mr. Raimi gestured toward the door and the reverend went inside.

"Let me grab you a drink, Reverend. A fruit punch with rum perhaps?" Mr. Raimi guessed and followed inside. "May I compliment your suit?"

Maya watched them pass and then pulled out the walkie talkie.

CHAPTER TWENTY-TWO

The call on the radio came through. "Blair is here," hissed Maya over the static. "Go now!"

Henry looked up from the radio and saw the waiting faces of the Midnight Pumpkin Society. All eager to begin.

"That's the word! What are we waiting for?" asked Hunter. "It's now or never!"

"We know what we have to do. Tonight, we shall bring back Halloween for the whole town. The risk may mean Sunday school for the next year, but it'll be worth it," Henry said, addressing his army. "We need to cover as much ground as possible. Some of us will take White Hart Lane, that'll be tricky being so close to the adults. Others will take Castle Street and the rest of us will cover Proctor Street. We all have our things to do and don't forget time is against us. We only have as long as Maya's mum and Mr. Raimi can keep the adults away. My Grandpa Ray will stay here for us when we need to get more decorations."

There was a wave of excitement and mischief and they all donned their masks.

By dim moonlight shrouded by grey clouds, the Midnight Pumpkin Society leaped, ran, jogged, raced, climbed, and jumped all across the town of Port Hampton.

Each kid setting in motion their part of the plan.

Hunter Tapert threw the toilet paper he had meticulously used typewriter ink from his father's office to draw a million black bats and cats on. He tossed them high up into all the trees in the front yards of Castle Street. Up and down, up and down, up and down. Giant arcs hanging from every branch. The beautiful streamers hung like the wrappings of an ancient mummy from an Egyptian tomb.

Hunter wore the ghastly face of a vampire.

Kelly Krug had spent the summer going through neighbour's gardens stealing the odd bedsheet from unguarded clotheslines. Though they were annoyed, most of the grown-ups simply bought new sheets and forgot about the missing ones. Slowly, over the months, Kelly had accumulated nearly thirty clean white bedsheets. She drew on silent screams of phantoms and stuffed their heads with newspaper giving the spirits their shape. Castle Street was haunted by phantoms. Her wandering, lost spooky spectres.

Kelly wore the mythical grimace of a gargoyle.

Charlotte May took like a flash down White Hart Lane, climbing every lamppost. As she reached the top, she ran a thick paint brush of orange paint down along the already black pole. Halloween candy canes that looked good enough to eat, dotted up and down the street. They would have been pumpkin and liquorice flavour and Charlotte couldn't help but smile at how they complemented Kelly's and Hunter's work.

Charlotte wore the ugly stare of a witch.

Henry flew down the paved street on his bicycle with both his front and back baskets full of papier-mâché Jack-O'-Lanterns. Eight in each basket. All of them the size of the happy birthday balloons from Mr. Raimi's store.

Each 'pumpkin' painted bright orange with black features that looked deep and hollow.

Henry had removed the playing cards from his wheel spokes and now glided silently and carefree. Stopping at one end of the street, he checked the houses for any lights. They had been undetected up until that point, but a mistake could expose the whole game.

No lights. They were still undercover and unseen.

Henry snuck up to front porches and front doors and gently placed one of his 'pumpkins' down. The fact it wouldn't be able to hold a candle was unimportant. It was more than just a pumpkin. It was a symbol. Nothing was more identifiable with the beautiful and honoured day of Halloween than a Jack-O'-Lantern, be it an actual pumpkin or, the best the society could manage, papier-mâché. Up and down the street, Henry crept like a strange All Hallows' Eve Santa Claus dropping off a present for the unsuspecting.

Henry wore the vacant face of a skull.

There was still much work to do.

The other kids followed behind hanging paper bats from every possible ledge and hook. Some hung orange fairy lights giving the night a twinkle. Some sprinkled candy on front porches ready for trick or treating and others scattered clay skeleton bones and cotton spider webs.

It was as if Halloween had never left.

Henry stood watching the society run around decorating. It filled him with joy, pride, and excitement but not just that. It was a different kind of joy felt only on this most special of nights. All Hallows Eve. He wished he could bottle the feeling to save for a harsh winter or a blazing summer. But for now, as Port Hampton became Halloween Town, he soaked up as much of the night as he could.

Two hours after they started, the radio walkie

talkie came to life on Henry's belt.

"You guys should see this. Blair is drunk!" said Maya over the radio.

CHAPTER TWENTY-THREE

Maya and Zimmy moved through the crowd of adults to try and see Blair. There had been radio silence for an hour and a half, but they knew Henry and the other kids were at work.

Maya looked over at Blair. Mr. Raimi and the reverend had been in a sort of drinking match. As soon as Blair had finished his drink of fruit punch with rum, Mr Raimi would quickly refill it with a huge smile and eagerness. For every drink Mr. Raimi had, the reverend would have two! And now, Blair sat on his own at a table with a loose tie and a drink in his hand, burped and looked around the room.

Maya clicked the radio. "Blair is drunk. He can barely stand up."

Watching the reverend, they saw Mr. Raimi approach. He gave the two spy youths a wink.

"Enjoying yourself Reverend?" Mr. Raimi asked.

The reverend stood and swayed. "I'm

having…a wonderful time…You've done a wonderful job…" The reverend burped again. "Excuse me."

"I'm glad you're having fun, I…" Mr. Raimi began.

"You know it's nice to see everyone here. Even you Raimi. I know…I would have thought you'd go to that synagogue but, you're welcome at my church."

Mr. Raimi held back his laugher. The once mean bulldog Blair was now as weak as a pussy cat.

"Thank you, Reverend," Mr. Raimi gritted his teeth.

"But… I still had you down as an enemy you know… why when you walked out on that service… I thought you would be against me."

"No… I…"

"It looks like I won," the reverend giggled. "No more Halloween! I couldn't be happier. Such a wicked thing to celebrate. Why those…stupid kids and their costumes and pumpkins. I've never cared for it. A silly thing."

Blair slumped down into his seat and steadied himself with another gulp of rum laced fruit punch… "All those kiddies locked up on their precious night…. it's too delicious."

Maya felt angry, her small hands shaking, but remained out of sight.

"And ya know what?" The reverend stood quickly. "I found out about those kids plan too."

Though Blair was drunk, Mr. Raimi knew not to underestimate him.

A grim grin spread across the reverend's face.

"I found their little stockpile. All those papier-mâché pumpkin things and dyed toilet paper, all those bedsheets… but… I went back with people…and it was all gone…" The reverend sounded sad as he hiccupped. "I bet those kids are still up to something… and I think…"

"What?" asked Mr. Raimi.

The reverend pointed an unsteady finger. "I think you're up to something too… and by the Lord… I'll figure it out."

Another hiccup. Blair slumped back into his chair.

Mr. Raimi stayed cool as a cucumber.

Blair gave a funny look.

"Well," Mr. Raimi stood. "I best go mingle. I'll bring you another drink, Reverend. Fruit punch again?"

Blair held up his glass but kept the look of suspicion on his face and burped.

CHAPTER TWENTY-FOUR

Henry looked down at his wristwatch. It was nearly nine P.M., three more hours of Halloween. They were nearly finished. White Hart Line was covered, as was Proctor Street and now the society met at the top of Castle Street, each kid out of breath but still pumped with adrenaline. They all wore their mischievous smiles under their masks and were ready to continue. The dark October night embraced them.

It was just how he had imagined it. It was truly his dream Halloween.

Blair, drunk and sitting in the town hall, had nearly been defeated.

"We have one more place to do," said Henry with a wicked smile.

"Where?" asked the other kids in unison.

"The vicarage. Blair's house."

The Midnight Pumpkin Society ran with all their might and gusto toward the vicarage. It would be the perfect full stop to the evening to decorate the Blair's house, really rub Blair's big nose in it.

They reached the still and quiet castle ruins and then went further inside to the church Lync gate. It was eerily calm, but they felt safe and confident.

"Right, Hunter, you still got some T.P?"" asked Henry, looking over the vicarage, trying to figure out the best course of action.

Hunter held up his half full duffel bag. "Yep! Plenty left, let's T.P it. See how Blair likes that."

"I still have some bedsheet ghosts, maybe four or five," said Kelly, digging into her bag.

"I have four Jack-O'-Lanterns left," counted Henry.

"But I bet you didn't know we had this," said Charlotte. She then proceeded to pull out a large, folded bedsheet. "This is the cherry on top."

Just as Henry and Charlotte began to unfold the surprise, the vicarage doors slowly opened.

In a panic, the children quickly dove behind the bushes, fearful they had been caught.

Henry clicked the radio. "Maya? Maya? You there?"

After a few seconds, there was a reply. "Yeah, we're here…"

"Where's Blair?" Henry asked urgently, eyeing the open door.

A hiss on the radio. "Blair is here, asleep."

Henry couldn't help but chuckle a little.

Peeking up from behind the bush, the light was so bright from the doors they couldn't adjust their eyes to see the figure at first then slowly the light and their eyes adjusted.

It was Elizabeth Blair.

"Hello?" she said quietly, looking out at the front garden.

The society remained silent.

Elizabeth started walking towards them.

"How's the plan going?" she asked, making her way up to the bushes.

The question threw Henry. He stepped out from behind the bush.

"We're nearly done…what are you doing here?" he asked.

"I was waiting," she replied.

"Waiting for what?"

"For you guys to come. I still want to help you," she said.

She held out her hand and, in the darkness, Henry could just about make out what she held in her open palm.

Keys.

"I took these from my dad," she said, offering Henry the keys.

Henry looked on puzzled.

"Don't do it Henry," warned Hunter. "Remember what she did, she told about The Den."

Elizabeth's deep blue eyes were honest.

"I don't think she did…no kid would take this risk," Henry said, taking the offered keys.

"We can decorate the vicarage, inside and out," Elizabeth said. "I told you, I'm not the rat, you have to believe me. I love Halloween."

Henry looked at the hopeful girl. Her eyes spoke of the truth and Henry felt they had acted too quickly to banish her from the society. But, on the other hand, she was the kid closest to Blair…On the third hand, she HAD just given Henry the keys to the vicarage. Weighing up those thoughts in his mind, Henry knew he had made the wrong decision to banish her. The rat in the society would remain unknown, though at this point there was no stopping their plan.

"Elizabeth Blair," he began in a loud voice so everyone could hear. "I hereby induct you back into the Midnight Pumpkin Society."

Elizabeth raised her hand like a scout and smiled.

Kelly pushed forward. "Enough talk. Come on, we're running out of time."

And so, the society, along with their new member, decorated the vicarage with everything they had left; ghosts, bones, bats, cobwebs, streamers and pumpkins, and dyed toilet paper. They laughed and giggled, thinking of how Blair would react when he saw.

As they were nearly finished, Charlotte pulled out the folded bed sheet with Hunter's help. She unfolded it to reveal a giant smiling Jack-O'-Lantern with, in big purple letters, 'HAPPY HALLOWEEN!' written across it.

"What a piece of art," said Henry as he ran to the opposite side of the pulpit. They hung the sheet on the stone edging of the cottage, and it spread out like a banner, a perfect Halloween backdrop.

It was then, that Henry knew their masterpiece was complete. It hardly mattered if they were caught now. They had done it.

A hiss came over the radio. Maya's delicate voice. "I think we might have a problem…the adults are getting ready to leave!"

CHAPTER TWENTY-FIVE

Zimmy whispered over his shoulder to Maya. "The adults are getting ready to leave, those guys better be ready."

And just as Zimmy said, the adults started picking up their coats from the back of their chairs and began wishing each other a goodnight. Every adult full to the brim with merry cocktails, each adult happy and friendly through booze-coloured glasses.

Maya moved through the crowd towards Dawn and tugged at her dress.

"We need more time," Maya whispered up to her mother. "I don't know if they others are finished!"

Dawn thought on her feet and quickly grabbed a half empty glass of wine from a nearby table.

"Folks, everyone… two minutes…" Dawn called out.

She was making it up off the top of her head.

Some adults murmured, others turned their heads.

Dawn smiled, trying to look casual. "I just want to… I want to thank Mr. Raimi…"

The crowd was dizzy and fuzzy. She was losing them to too many cocktails.

"I just want to thank Mr. Raimi for throwing such a wonderful party…"

"Where is ol' Sam anyways?" asked a voice.

"I ain't seen him all night," another voice said.

A snore rose above the crowd and all heads turned toward the sound.

Blair was slumped over the table, drink still clutched in his hand. Drunk and asleep. He had drunk a whole bottle of rum! The adults chuckled and laughed, like children.

"And we all appreciate Blair's support," the voice said from the doors.

It was Mr. Raimi, with a huge smile across his face. "And now, as the night comes to a close, I have a surprise for you all."

Excited whispers amongst the crowd. Each adult, best friends with their neighbour in their merry state.

"What surprise?" said a voice.

"What could it be?" said another.

"Oh, I love a surprise," said a woman.

Mr. Raimi threw open the front doors and let

in the night.

The adults gasped at the sights before them.

HALLOWEEN!   SAMHAIN!   ALL HALLOWS EVE!

Wondrous and spooky Halloween decorations, swaying in the gentle autumn breeze. A beautiful sight to behold.

Mr. Raimi climbed upon a bench and stood above the crowd. "Remember! Feel the wonder in the air, Halloween is here!"

More laughs and whispers amongst the crowd.

"Remember the joy, the fun, the mischief. Remember the excitement as a child yourself. Excitement for Halloweens past. It was our night to live and to breath. We used to scare ourselves to know we were alive. Alive and Happy! Who here doesn't miss age old Trick or Treating? Or bobbing for apples? Even dressing up in costumes, some store bought, some homemade. We all looked forward to Halloween more than Christmas and Easter combined," Mr. Raimi called out with arms outstretched.

"It's a magical time where we can let our inner child run free. An inner child that's been lost to mortgages, jobs, and the dreary day to day life of being a grown up. Don't forget that special inner child longing for a good Halloween night. These kids, these wonderful, amazing kids, have given us the best Halloween since we can remember. They've given us a chance to feel those feelings once again and to relive our memories…So what can I say but: HAPPY HALLOWEEN!"

Mr. Krug stumbled toward one of the bedsheet ghosts, his eyes bright. "Why, I used to make ghosts just like this as a kid."

"Me too," said a few more voices in the crowd.

Jim Hall's dad nodded. "Oh, how I remember…what a great time."

"Oh, and look, pumpkins!" said Mrs. Hall, swaying on her feet. "Oh, how clever!"

Slowly, there were more cheers and happy talks in the giddy crowd, full of wine and cocktails as they gazed upon the decorations filling the streets.

"Oh Dear, don't you remember Halloweens as a kid? Wasn't it fun," Mr. Tapert said to his wife, who was close to falling asleep.

The adult's nostalgia came flooding back with good memories they were sure they had forgotten. Maybe it was the cocktails in them or some strange and special October pollen on the air.

"Don't fall under Blair's spell. Remember people!" Mr. Raimi called out. "Remember the magic and excitement of Halloween. It's precious, too precious to die."

And the adults walked the streets full of spirit and spirits. All were warm and happy. They celebrated for they remembered the magic, even just for that one October night.

Across the street, Mr. Raimi caught view of Henry, Maya and the other kids standing on the corner of White Hart Lane and Proctor Street.

The adults were full of nostalgic dreams.

"Yes, I remember!" said a voice.

"Oh, the memories." remembered another.

"Yes, we lost it but now we have it back!" said yet another.

The memories and the past came flooding back, filling their minds with special thoughts and memories. Wither they would remember such thoughts tomorrow once the drinks had worn off was irrelevant. By then it would be November and Halloween would be safe in bed for another year.

"Happy Halloween," said a voice.

"Yes! Happy Halloween," said another.

Mr. Raimi jogged to the street corner and embraced the children.

"You did it guys, you really did it!" and he smiled and cried with joy. "Happy Halloween, guys!"

CHAPTER TWENTY-SIX

As the adults cheered and laughed and looked on with wide eyed wonder, the children of Port Hampton celebrated their Halloween.

Among the spooky and joyous celebrations, Henry and Maya walked the streets admiring their masterpiece and knew with full happy hearts that Blair had lost.

A gentle mist began to fall from the sky, delicate and silky, like glitter in the orange hum of the streetlights.

"Do you think there will ever be another Halloween like this?" Maya asked as they climbed the fence outside the Cowan's house.

Henry settled on the wooden fence and looked out at the beautiful street. "I don't know…but there will always be Halloween and we'll always celebrate it, even when we're as old as these guys."

Maya slid her hand across the fence and wrapped her small fingers around Henry's hand.

"I think you may be right."

They held hands and smiled.

Across the street, Henry could see his Grandpa Ray, full of October spirits, handing out candy to trick or treaters and giving congratulations to their costumes and masks.

Henry hadn't seen his Grandpa Ray smile that way in a long time.

Henry Crane and Maya Fox sat on the fence, enjoying the last precious chills of October before midnight and the end of Halloween 1993.

ACKNOWLEDGEMENTS

So many people over the years have helped and supported me when I told them I was going to be a writer and for that I want to thank them.

Camille: for years of support and love and putting up with constant clanking of the typewriter.

Eric: for taking me to Green Town (Waukegan) Illinois for a cool glass of Dandelion Wine.

Sam: for chasing scarecrows with me.

Lara: for reading every draft of the book and loving each one. My dear October friend.

Scott: for being my storytelling partner in crime for so many years.

Aaron: for being the cool kid and making me feel like one too.

Lewis: for being the voice of reason and logic when I doubted myself.

Thanks to my family. I love you all.

And a huge thank you to John Katzenbach for being a friend, mentor and a therapist.